Up a Road Slowly

I thought about things Aunt Cordelia and I had talked about that evening. Especially love. I wondered if I would ever love anyone; if any boy would ever love me. I wondered what it would be like to have a boy's kiss—oh, not that silly kid-play of Danny's when Chris and Jimmy held my arms. What interested me were the kisses I read about or the ones I had watched with a kind of hypnotized distaste when I had seen them in the movies. I wondered what it was like to be married, and then I wondered about babies. I wanted a baby very much, one that was all mine, beautiful and soft. I wanted to be grown up and to know all about the things I wondered about. I sighed and turned in my bed luxuriously. "I do so want to be complete," I thought.

Up a Road Slowly

by Irene Hunt

TEMPO BOOKS, NEW YORK

This **Tempo Book** contains the complete
text of **the original** hardcover edition.
It has **been completely** reset in a typeface
designed for **easy reading**, and was printed
from new film.

UP A ROAD SLOWLY

A Tempo Book/published by arrangement with
Follett Publishing Company

PRINTING HISTORY
Tempo edition / January 1974
Fourteenth printing / January 1983

ISBN: 0-441-85459-1

Tempo Books are published by Charter Communications, Inc.
200 Madison Avenue, New York, New York 10016.
Tempo Books are registered in the United States Patent Office.
PRINTED IN THE UNITED STATES OF AMERICA

To Beulah, Shirley, and Freda

Up a Road
Slowly

Chapter One

Three children stood outside our gate in the bright October sunlight, silent and still as figurines in a gift shop window, watching each step I took as I came slowly down the flagstone walk across the lawn. I was still weak from the same sickness that had stricken my mother, and it had been many days since I had played with any of the neighborhood children. There was a strong breeze that afternoon, and I remember how a brown oak leaf floated down and rested upon the red hair of the only boy in the group. It was funny; that shining leaf looked like a girl's hair-bow on a boy's head. For a few seconds I almost forgot the feeling of bewilderment and desolation within me, and I wanted to laugh at the silly look of a boy with a huge, flat hair-bow on his red head. I didn't, though; I remembered quickly that it was not a day for laughter.

We stared at one another in the blank manner of young children confronted by uncertainty. As late as the hot, dry days of August we had played with one another, but now they saw me touched with a sorrow unknown to them, and I was suddenly a stranger. Their solemn faces reflected the warning of their mothers: "You must be very kind to Julie—very kind—"

The smallest of the three finally spoke. She was a child of five or so; she had a high, piping voice, and there was a look of determination about her as if she had suddenly decided to get at the bottom of a piece of mysterious gossip. "You're not going to live here anymore, are you?" It was actually more nearly a statement than a question. "We hear that you're going to live with your aunt in the country."

That is when I began to scream. I knew that there was something terribly wrong inside our house, but I hadn't known that something was about to drive me from my home. There had been many people in the house for the past two days; my aunt Cordelia was there, our own family doctor and another strange one, many neighbors, all of them with grave, white faces. "Adam hasn't said a word," I heard someone whisper. "He only sits and stares." That was Father they were talking about. There had been another whisper. "The doctor says that Julie is near hysteria; you must watch over your little sister carefully, Laura."

There was a stillness all through the house in spite of the activity. I had sat for a long time in Mother's little sewing room that afternoon, and had watched the wind whip great wrinkles in the white sheets that hung on the line. The wrinkles had come to look strange to me as I watched them; they grinned at me, malicious, hateful grins.

The child who had spoken to me was frightened. I

hated her because I feared that what she said might be true, and so I screamed and would have struck her if I had been able to get beyond the gate. She grasped the hands of the two on either side of her and they scuttled away, frightened and outraged.

Then my brother, Christopher, who had followed me out to the gate called loudly for Laura, who was quickly beside me, speaking to me, lifting me in her arms. Laura was seventeen, beautiful, and my idol. It was she, rather than our frail mother or our father, a preoccupied and overworked professor, who was able to control a stubborn, somewhat overindulged little sister; many of my tantrums had been short-lived because of Laura. I would risk losing favor with almost anyone, but not with my sister.

She carried me up to her room overlooking the flower garden. The windows were open and the dry, bitter scents of autumn were in the air that stirred a curtain near the bed where Laura laid me. I vaguely wished that I could control the screaming that distressed Laura, but I was completely helpless.

The doctor came in after a while, I remember, and forced me to swallow a small pill with a little water. After that I went to sleep and while I slept, the prediction of little five-year-old-at-the-gate came true, for when I awoke the next morning, I was, indeed, at my aunt's house in the country, five miles out of the small college town where I had lived my first years. All the forebodings seemed to be coming true, and the bottom was surely falling out of my world.

Aunt Cordelia was not at home that morning, but a gentle, plump woman in blue gingham with a white apron tied at her waist was sitting beside the bed when I opened my eyes. I knew her slightly; she was

Mrs. Peters, and I knew that she and her husband had for many years managed the farm which Aunt Cordelia and Uncle Haskell owned jointly. She was a kind woman, but in my anxiety, her mannerisms irritated me; she smiled too continuously, and she avoided the pronoun "I" as if it were taboo.

"Now Mrs. Peters has a good breakfast ready for our little girl. Let's get dressed nicely and when our Julie has had a bite to eat she can go outside and play with the children Mrs. Peters has asked up here for the day. That will be lots of fun, now won't it?"

"I don't want to play," I said stonily, "and I don't want to eat breakfast."

Mrs. Peters did not comment upon that, but she clucked a great deal and made vague little remarks as she helped me to dress. "Now, our little socks and shoes," she said, "and now our pretty petticoat."

The drug in the doctor's pill had left me limp and somewhat out of touch with reality. I felt unreasonably critical of Mrs. Peters, but too tired for any further protests. We walked together down the curving staircase to the living room, through the dining room and out to Aunt Cordelia's kitchen where, again, there were children facing me with wide solemn eyes, children who knew something I didn't quite know, or wouldn't quite admit.

The boy was Danny Trevort, and the girl was Carlotta Berry. I liked Danny better, even that morning, although I had little reason for it beyond the fact that he talked less than the little girl.

"You're coming to our school, aren't you?" she asked after a breathless little speech of welcome which I now realize was learned by rote. "My mama says you'll be in my class because you're seven same as me—"

Then the woman was back, clucking softly again. "Now, now," she said, "let's think about a game we can play after we have our breakfast. Couldn't we play hide-and-seek, Danny? Wouldn't that be a fine game?"

The boy nodded gravely. "Sure, if the new girl wants to play," he said.

"No," I answered, and turning my back to them, I walked out of the kitchen, silently daring them to follow me. I had a feeling that the three of them watched me, uncertain of what to do next.

Aunt Cordelia's house was familiar, but at that time still awesome and forbidding to me. It was a large old house, set well back from the road in a grove of oak and white pine and stately elm; its twelve rooms were spacious and airy, a delight in summer and a monumental heating problem in winter. There was a wide veranda across the front of the house with tall white columns and a half dozen steps leading to a brick paved walk which curved in and out among the trees until it reached the big gate at the road.

There were evidences of prosperous years and tight ones, pressed shoulder to shoulder throughout the house. There were wide marble-topped fireplaces in the library, living room, and dining room, even in some of the bedrooms upstairs, but there was no central heating and in winter the beauty of the rooms downstairs was marred by great coal-burning stoves that too often belched black smoke when a damper was inadequately adjusted. There was a grand piano in the living room, an instrument bought with much sacrifice by my grandmother, who had fancied that her eldest son, my Uncle Haskell, was destined for the world of music. The great, gleaming piano deserved a Persian rug or at least a parquet floor beneath it; instead, it stood upon a rag carpet made on a country loom, as simple a bit of tapestry as might have been found in any country home in the years of Aunt Cordelia's youth. It was my aunt's grim, reality-facing answer to her mother's wastefulness.

The rooms upstairs held fear for me during my early childhood. Half of Aunt Cordelia's life had been spent in caring for her aged mother and two spinster aunts, and one of these latter, a tiny gray wisp of a woman, I had encountered once when I had wandered upstairs on a tour of exploration. I had opened a door tentatively in order to peek inside, when a woman turned in her chair and smiled toothlessly at me.

"Whose little girl are you?" she quavered, and I stood there for a few seconds, numb with fear and saying nothing. Then as I fled down the hall I heard a dreadful little cackle of laughter following me, and I nearly fell head-long as my feet raced down the stairs. It was a long time before the small gray presence was exorcised from the otherwise pleasant rooms of Aunt Cordelia's second floor.

Uncle Haskell lived in a renovated carriage house out back. There were a number of reasons why he preferred the privacy of his own establishment, one of which may have been the desire to save himself the distress of seeing his sister carry the load of responsibility which he had no intention of sharing. He liked drinking in private, too; it was easier to maintain the myth of a cultivated taste for an occasional glass of fine wine or some exotic beverage from a foreign port, since he did not relish the image of himself as a common drunkard. He once told my brother, Chris, and me that the bottles we found on the shelves of his kitchen held rare wines from the sunny vineyards of France, and we were impressed until Chris, who was able to read, pointed out that the labels bore the blunt English words, "Old Crow." Naturally, said Uncle Haskell. The French are a very obliging people. They placed the English translation of *Le Vieux Corbeau* on bottles destined for America.

He was a handsome man, this uncle who was both an alcoholic and a pathological liar. His face at fifty-five was unlined, and his skin instead of showing the ravages of alcohol, was youthfully fresh and clear. His blue eyes, large and heavily lashed, were full of innocent good humor, a kind of bland assurance that all the world loved him and believed in him. He had a thick growth of wavy, golden hair which he wore rather longer than did the men who were our neighbors, and he kept it immaculate and shining at all times. He was slender and supple; when he walked it was as if he heard an inner music that delighted him down to his heels.

Uncle Haskell had had reason to be furious with Chris and me once in our very early years, and at that time he had borne himself with a magnanimity which somehow impressed me. We had found in Aunt Cordelia's basement a box containing twelve large bottles of a beautifully colored red-gold liquid bearing the English translation of *Le Vieux Corbeau*, although at that time we were too young to read it. The size and shape of the bottles had suggested bowling pins to me. Chris, to his credit, had said no to the game which I suggested, but after I had kicked a couple of bottles from an inverted washtub onto the concrete floor and we had waded in triumph through pools of richly fragrant liquid and had splashed one another lightly, he could not resist joining me in the demolition of another bottle. By the time we were apprehended, five of Uncle Haskell's bottles lay broken on the basement floor.

Mother had been appalled and chagrined. She apologized stiffly to Uncle Haskell, for she was torn between shame at the destructiveness of her children and a conviction that at least a sizable amount of her brother's whiskey was where it belonged.

Uncle Haskell, leaning gracefully in the doorway, turned a look of mingled pain and amusement upon the two culprits and then placed a comforting arm around Mother's shoulders.

"Don't fret your pretty head for another minute, little Ethel," he said, knowing well that Father would repay him for his loss. "No doubt we should feel a certain measure of gratitude at being able to contribute to the innocent pleasures of childhood." He patted her gently and then added, looking me full in the eye, "Next time, let's leash your brats, shall we?"

All that was long ago and far away from the October morning when I first came to live with Aunt Cordelia. The memories came back in little pieces as I walked through the large, high-ceilinged rooms, hurrying through them with only one purpose: to get away from Mrs. Peters and the two children. There was a place I remembered, the closet under the stairs that led from the attic to the second floor.

Chris and I had played there once, half afraid, half fascinated by the dimly lighted cavern in which the ceiling followed the line of the descending stairs, becoming so low toward the back that even a young child had not room to sit upright. I found the entrance and hesitated; the place looked grim and forbidding, but for all that, it offered security to a small bewildered animal wanting to lick its wounds in solitude. I got down on my hands and knees and crawled as far back into the musty smelling shadows as my height would permit. There I rested against a pile of neatly packaged bedding, finding little comfort in loneliness, but preferring it to the company of the other children.

Mrs. Peters discovered me before long and she stood at the door, pleading, cajoling and finally threatening a little.

"Now, let's be a good girl, Julie; come out and let the sun shine on you for a while. Mrs. Peters won't insist that you play if you don't want to—just come out and get a breath of good fresh air. This place will give our Julie a bad headache."

But I wouldn't budge, not even when she bribed me with chocolate cake. And when she finally started to crawl into the closet in order to pull me out by force, I screamed in such a way that she must have been frightened. Finally she placed some food at the entrance of the closet and left me for the rest of the morning and early afternoon.

I lay there in the darkness for hour after hour with no clear-cut understanding of what my sorrow was; there was a sense of helplessness as to what was going to happen to me, a sense of bewilderment, and the aching memory of yesterday's white faces, the whispers, and the little girl who said, "You're not going to live here anymore, are you?"

I must have slept at last and when I wakened there were voices outside my hiding place and shadows of long legs, sweeping dresses. After a while they moved away, and only two were left, two whom I recognized by their voices. They were Mrs. Peters and Aunt Cordelia.

"I tried half the morning, Cordelia," I heard Mrs. Peters saying earnestly, and it struck me that she did, after all, know how to use the word "I." "I coaxed and begged and once I started in to get her, but my lands, she screamed like a child gone daft. I tell you the truth, I was afraid she might go into a spasm. I hope you don't think I've done wrong."

Then Aunt Cordelia's voice, low and very calm. "No, Cora, you did right. I am grateful to you for staying with her, very grateful." She paused and then got down on her knees preparatory to crawling back into the closet toward me. "I'll see to her. You can go fix coffee for the others if you will be so kind."

I was afraid of Aunt Cordelia Bishop, not that she had ever been unkind, but there was an aloofness about her that had always made her keep a considerable distance between us. Chris liked her, and he was obviously her favorite, a fact which didn't interest me especially, for with me Aunt Cordelia simply didn't count. I had once overheard Father telling someone that "Cordelia and the little one bristle at one another in almost exactly the same manner." Perhaps we did. I hadn't been aware of it, but on that October afternoon she was the last person in the world I wanted to see crawling toward me in the depths of the dark closet.

When she was near me she spoke the name by which she, alone, called me. I had been baptized "Julie," but Aunt Cordelia felt that certain feminine names ending in "ie" or "y" indicated a frivolity of which she disapproved. Thus, among her pupils, a small Elsie became "Elsa," and a Betty had to answer to a stern "Elizabeth." She had told Mother that "Julie" was simply a sloppy pronunciation of that fine old Roman name which their paternal grandmother had borne. And so Aunt Cordelia called me "Julia."

"Yes, Aunt Cordelia," I answered, just a little above a whisper. Mother had seen to it that I was always polite to Aunt Cordelia whether I liked her or not.

She came a little nearer to me, and leaning forward, put her arms around me and drew me to her lap. My head was against her cheek, and when I sobbed, I could feel the trembling of Aunt Cordelia's body, and I knew that her face was wet with tears as mine was.

That was the one time I have ever known her to cry, and it was the first time I remember her holding me in her arms. We sat in the dark closet together for a long time; then when there were no more tears left, we crawled out and began our decade together.

Chapter Two

To be suddenly catapulted into a new way of life at seven is very hard. I envied Laura; she, at least, had our old home, her own rose and cream-colored room, the closets full of Mother's dresses. She had Father, too, and the good smell of his cigar in his study; she ate her meals in the same old dining room with him, went to school with the young people she had always known. I thought that life was much kinder to Laura than to Christopher and me.

What I didn't realize was that at seventeen, Laura did not have the adaptability, the readiness to forget, that Christopher and I had at seven and nine. We thought of Mother often in the early days of our new life; sometimes we cried when we were homesick for times that were gone, for the old sense of security within our family. But the days slipped by and the memory of Mother grew fainter, the rooms of the old house that had once been awesome and fearful became familiar and pleasant; school had its compensations, Uncle Haskell was a huge joke, and Aunt Cordelia was a challenge.

Aunt Cordelia was our teacher as well as our guardian. At the small white schoolhouse where she had taught since she was a young girl, she was *only* our teacher; she gave no sign of knowing us any better than the other children. We called her "Miss Cordelia" as the others did, and when she stood behind her desk, slender and erect in her plain tailored suit with her rich brown and gray hair coiled in braids about her head, we looked at her with the proper respect she expected of us. She demanded obedience, but she was not a grim teacher; if we read a gay story that brought laughter to us, we could count on Aunt Cordelia's appreciation too. She read aloud to us on Friday afternoons, and she read beautifully; I came very close to loving Aunt Cordelia during those long afternoons when I rested my arms upon the desk in front of me and became acquainted with Jim Hawkins and Huck Finn, with little David and Goliath, with Robinson Crusoe on his island, and with the foolish gods and their kinfolk somewhere above the clouds on Mount Olympus. She could be very stern about some misdemeanor in the classroom, but when her point had been made, she seemed to forget the matter entirely and became a pleasant, forgiving friend. Sometimes it was a gambling matter to predict Aunt Cordelia's reactions.

Ordinarily, Chris and I walked the mile and a half to school with our aunt, shoulders pushed well back, every breath employing the use of our diaphragms, our minds fixed, at Aunt Cordelia's suggestion, on the beauty of Nature and the glory of the firmament. On especially inclement mornings Aunt Cordelia would drive her precious car, which was almost as shining and beautiful as it had been ten years earlier. We loved driving to school in style, but our pleasure soon became dimmed a little by the fact that we knew we must spend an hour or so that evening in washing and polishing the car before it was put away for Sunday and holiday driving.

Aunt Cordelia didn't really have to teach for a livelihood; the income from the farm was sufficient for her needs, and the modest salary she received for each month of the school year was not the incentive which brought her back to her desk year after year. Her reason for teaching was actually the belief that no one else would do the work quite so well, would understand the backgrounds of these children whose parents she had taught when she was young. There was never a doubt in Aunt Cordelia's mind but that *her* teaching was the best to be had, and she would have felt that she was denying something beyond price to the handful of country children who sat in her classroom, if she allowed a younger or a less dedicated woman to take over.

And so she went back year after year, teaching from nine until four o'clock, then sweeping and dusting the room after school, carrying in great buckets of coal to bank the fire for the night, arriving at school an hour early on Monday mornings during the winter months in order to get the fire started and the room warm before the children arrived.

Twice a year, in the fall and again in spring, we got a half holiday during which time we helped Aunt

Cordelia wash and polish the windows, scrub the floor, wash and wax the desks. By the time Danny Trevort and Chris were ten, they had, of their own accord, taken over the task of carrying in the coal of an evening. Often the three of us stayed after school and did the sweeping and dusting for her, I with a big apron protecting my school dress and one of Aunt Cordelia's round dust caps protecting my hair. She never failed to thank us for our help, and now and then, as a special treat, Danny would be asked to spend the evening with us and there would be a weiner roast or a fried chicken dinner in payment for our janitorial services.

Aunt Cordelia did pretty well at treating all her pupils with the same impersonal detachment, but sometimes she was hard put to hide a particular warmth which she felt toward both Danny Trevort and my brother, Chris. They were both rosy, smooth-cheeked little boys, mischievous at times, but frank and honest, sharing a respect for Aunt Cordelia which I did not always feel. Sometimes at night, when Chris was bent over his homework, Aunt Cordelia would let her hand rest for a second on his head and when he looked up, they would smile at one another. I felt very alone and lost when they did that; sometimes I felt very angry too. As for Danny, he was the one child in school whom Aunt Cordelia addressed by his diminutive name. It is true that he had been baptized "Daniel," and Aunt Cordelia had as little patience with pet names as she had for most feminine names ending in "ie" or "y"; still, for some unaccountable reason she broke with her principles in his case: he was always "Danny" Trevort.

Most of us carried our lunches in tin pails. Carlotta Berry had a basket with daisies painted all over the lid, which set her apart socially. We ate out under the trees when it was at all possible; in all the years I never became quite reconciled to eating inside with the smell of dust and winter garments and many kinds of food.

The problem of eating lunch with Aggie Kilpin was one of sharp annoyance to me for a long time, but by the end of my first year in the new school, I had found the solution.

Aggie was a mistreated, undernourished and retarded girl, the youngest child of a shiftless, vicious father and a mother who had been beaten down by the cruelties of her life. Aggie must have been ten or eleven the first winter that I knew her and even then, she hardly recognized a dozen words in the primer from which Aunt Cordelia tried to teach her. She would stand beside my aunt's desk floundering through a page that the youngest child in the room could have read with ease, and after each mistake, looking around the room to grin and smirk as if her failures were evidences of some bit of cleverness on her part. It was dreadful to watch her; I averted my eyes from Aggie whenever possible.

But it was not Aggie's retardedness that made her a pariah among us; it was the fact that she stank to high Heaven. Aunt Cordelia had pled with the girl for years to treat herself to an occasional tub of soapy water, to shampoo her hair, to wash just once in a while the shabby dress which she wore every day of the year. Aggie would grimace and mouth some half-intelligible garble, but she never lost any of her over-ripe fragrance. Aunt Cordelia stopped trying to do anything about it after a while; as a matter of fact, she thought it quite possible that Aggie's family might have turned upon her if the girl had shown any disposition to be different.

I loathed poor Aggie, who seemed to have a perfect gift for making herself repulsive. She stood at the blackbload one day, I remember, and before the entire school used a word that all of us had been brought up to consider dirty. It was a slip of the tongue with poor Aggie, but I was shocked. Some of the big boys laughed. Danny didn't, and neither did my brother; they sat side by side studying the pages of their geography with frowning intensity and very red faces. None of the girls laughed except Carlotta, who didn't want to, but became hysterical and had to go outside to the pump and wash her face until she got hold of herself.

Then Aunt Cordelia demanded "Silence," whereupon silence descended upon the room. Everybody was ashamed except Aggie; she was not accustomed to being the center of attention, and she threw sly glances at the boys who had laughed, preening herself a little at the success of something she had done, a something of which she was completely unconscious.

I used this incident to convince Aunt Cordelia that Aggie was no proper companion for the rest of us, who were considerably younger, that we had every right to shun her company. But Aunt Cordelia was not convinced. She saw to it that Aggie was included in all of our games, and what was hardest for us to bear, that Aggie was invited to join our little circle at lunchtime. Sometimes we would try sneaking away hurriedly at noon; inevitably we would hear a stern, "Julia—Elsa—Carlotta, I believe that you girls have forgotten to invite Agnes to go with you."

And so we would have to ask her, and Aggie would come galloping eagerly, usually to *my* side because I was Aunt Cordelia's niece, and she seemed to know that I was under special pressure to be a decently behaving classmate. She called me "kid," and she would throw her arm around my neck until I learned to dodge. Then when we were seated under the trees she would take out unappetizing-looking food which usually smelled strongly of onion, and would eat noisily, laughing at everything that was said and inching nearer to my side each time I inched away from hers.

Finally I organized a seating arrangement and did not hesitate to use my prestige as Aunt Cordelia's niece in enforcing the rules.

"We will sit in a big circle," I explained, "and the Queen will sit in the middle. Aggie is the oldest so she gets to be the Queen. The rest of us are subjects, and we are not allowed to look at the Queen while she eats, so of course, we will have to sit with our backs to her. Do you know, Aggie, that you could have us beheaded if we dared to look at you while you were eating?"

Aggie *didn't* know, and she didn't much enjoy her royal role after the first day or two. She wanted Lottie or Elsie to be the Queen—*not* Julie, because she wanted to be a peasant at Julie's side. But we were adamant. "You are the oldest, Aggie. It wouldn't be right for one of us to be the Queen." And again, "Shame on you, Aggie; you ought to be proud that we are letting you be our Queen."

The circle of peasants grew wider and wider as the days went by until our poor unlovely Queen sat in splendid isolation where she could not offend her subjects.

Aunt Cordelia discovered our game one day. We explained it to her with the same wide-eyed innocence that we had feigned when we explained it to Aggie. For a minute I was unsure; I thought I saw a storm approaching. But Aunt Cordelia was silent. She stood looking at us for a little while and, although I was pretty young, I detected amusement, sadness, and a kind of baffled uncertainty in her look. Finally she turned away without saying anything.

In the months before Danny and Chris and I were old enough to help Aunt Cordelia with her janitorial work, the three of us walked with Carlotta, Elsie Devers, and Jimmy Ferris down the road from school each evening. We ranged in age from seven to ten; Elsie and Jimmy were the two oldest and a little superior in their attitude because they knew about the intricacies of decimal fractions; Lottie was the prettiest, Chris was the tallest, I was the youngest and toughest, and Danny was the sweetest. I loved Danny secretly, or thought I did, but for all my love I didn't hesitate to hurt him one evening, an act that hurt *me* to remember for many years.

It started with Jimmy betting a million that Danny wouldn't dare kiss me, and Danny betting a million that he would, too, dare, all of which led to Chris and Jimmy pinning my arms behind me and Danny giving me a triumphant if unenthusiastic kiss. I was furious at all three of them, not so much because of the kiss as at the indignity of being thus kissed. It was Danny, however, who as soon as my arms were loosed, got the impact of a small hard fist that I had learned to use effectively as Chris could have testified. Danny's eye was swollen shut and rimmed with green and purple by the time we reached the big house in the grove and found Aunt Cordelia in her kitchen.

She bathed the eye of her favorite in cold water and held a silver spoon against the swollen flesh while she listened to the story of what happened. She said nothing at first, but after a while she quietly gave us her private opinion that a small boy's kiss was hardly in as poor taste as a small girl's physical violence. That, at least, was the gist of her remarks; after that she ignored me and asked Chris to go the rest of the way home with Danny and to apologize for his sister's behavior.

I slunk out to the surrounding woods, disgraced, heavyhearted and resentful. Public opinion was against me as I could see by the prim looks which Carlotta and Elsie bent upon me. I had hurt someone who was gentle and good, someone I loved, and that brought a heaviness to my throat. Aunt Cordelia, however, had blamed me and not any of the three boys; I resented that so much that it almost overcame my remorse.

There was a cluster of slender birches just beyond a thicket of blackberry vines, four silver-barked trees arranged in a rough semicircle with intertwining branches forming a leafy roof. I called this cluster of trees my cathedral, and I came there often when life's problems became particularly heavy. It was in this retreat that I found shelter on that spring evening after I punched Danny.

I knelt in what would have been true penitence if Aunt Cordelia's rebuff had not kindled so much rage, and I gave the Divine Presence all the details. I asked Him to consider the fact that three boys, all bigger than I was, were the ones who had started the trouble, and that a lady who pretended to be so dedicated to fair play had behaved in a way that no one, certainly not He, could call fair.

"Why is it," I demanded, "that Thou lettest these things always happen to *me*? Why dost Thou always let me be the one to get into trouble? I'd hate to think that Thou wert as unfair as Aunt Cordelia but it begins to look as if—"

I heard a slight stirring then, from behind one of the trees, and opening my eyes, saw Uncle Haskell, golf bag over his shoulder, leaning nonchalantly against one of the trees, laughter spread all over his face.

"You're snooping," I told him angrily. "I was trying to pray, and you have no right to snoop when someone is praying."

"I am *not* snooping, my darling niece, nor do I have the slightest interest in your prayers." He laid the golf bag aside and sat down in front of me. "As a matter of fact, however, you weren't actually praying you know. You were giving Jehovah a penny lecture."

I felt too depressed for an argument. When he asked me what the trouble was, I went through the story once again. "Aunt Cordelia isn't fair," I said finally. "She likes boys better than girls; it's as plain as anything. She likes Chris and Danny and even Jimmy Ferris better than she likes me."

Uncle Haskell laughed lightly. "The very trait she most resented in Mama. Ah, Cordelia!"

"You mean that my grandmother liked you better than Aunt Cordelia?"

"Naturally! I was male, beautiful, and brilliant; Cordelia was female, only so-so as to looks, bright enough, but certainly not scintillating."

"What about my mother?"

"Oh, Ethel was a rather charming child, but by the time she came along, Mama was so wrapped up in me that she was happy to leave Ethel's upbringing to Cordelia."

I sat for a time, tongue-tied with resentment. When I was finally able to speak at all, my protest was, even to my own ears, weak and inane.

"And do you really think that was right?" I asked, trying to put my anger into each syllable.

"My dear child, I couldn't care less as to whether it was right or not. All that concerns me is that I got the best of the bargain." He looked out at the shadowy woods, his clear blue eyes shining with what appeared to be perfect content. Then his brows suddenly shot up in sharp V-shapes. "Or did I?" he asked, still smiling, but somewhat more subdued. "I suppose that's debatable. Well, you'll have to ask your Aunt Cordelia. Or your father, the impeccable Adam."

"What do you mean—'impeccable'?" I demanded, getting ready to defend Father.

"Without defect. Faultless. Don't worry; Adam is so charmed by middle class values that he will accept 'impeccable' as a proper tribute. At least, I think so. And if he doesn't—" Uncle Haskell spread his beautiful, well-kept hands before him and took time to admire for a second the shining ovals of his nails. "It's strange," he added after a little, "that both of my sisters should have fallen in love with high-minded, irreproachable gentlemen, so different from their brother—and so immeasurably more pedestrian."

"Did Aunt Cordelia actually fall in love at one time?" I asked incredulously.

"My dear child, do you mean that a generation is growing up without having heard of Jonathan Eltwing? Certainly, your Aunt Cordelia fell in love—I am not sure that she has ever pulled herself out of it."

Jonathan Eltwing held no interest for me, nor did Aunt Cordelia's love life; however, new words held a fascination for me, and I was drawn to the word "impeccable." It had a good sound; moreover it meant without defect. Well, good. I did a quick bit of generalization based upon what I had heard of Uncle Haskell's heavy drinking and the ultimate ravages it was bound to bring to his system.

"Is your liver impeccable?" I asked pointedly.

Another man with his weakness might have been angered, but not Uncle Haskell. His laughter rang through the woods.

"My liver is in an enviable state of health and well-being, dear niece," he chortled. "Much to the consternation of all the prophets, my general health, including the condition of my liver is—yes, impeccable."

I felt that I had, perhaps, been a little rude. "I'm glad," I told him politely. "I hoped that your liver was impeccable."

"I'll just bet you did." He looked at me good-humoredly. "You evidently weren't as solicitous about young Trevort's health an hour ago as you are about mine. Are you quite sure that you didn't knock some teeth out?"

"I don't think so. Just his eye. Not out, but I made it black."

Uncle Haskell shook his head. "What Mama would have done to any brat who might have messed me up like that." He smiled to himself. "Dear Mama," he said, "dear, dear Mama."

I got the impression that he wasn't nearly as fond of Grandmother as the many "dears" might have indicated.

"If I ever have a boy, I'm going to see that he gets the blame for the things he does just as much as the girls do," I said.

"You're never going to get the chance to have a boy if you don't do something about that truculent little chin of yours." He got to his feet, hoisted the golf bag to his shoulder, and stooped to tweak my nose. "Accept the fact that this is a man's world and learn how to play the game gracefully, my sweet."

I watched him as he strode off with his characteristically buoyant step into the shadows. It occurred to me that there was no golf course within five miles, and that if there were, it would be too dark at that hour for a game; moreover, I suddenly realized that there were no clubs in the brown bag over Uncle Haskell's shoulder.

When I went back to the house at twilight, Aunt Cordelia looked at me thoughtfully, and her voice was kinder than it had been when she passed judgment on me earlier.

"The boys certainly have their share of blame for this unfortunate episode, Julia," she said. "I feel that I erred when I placed all the blame on you this afternoon."

My heart warmed to her in a sudden rush of love.

I wondered if she had remembered how her mother always favored Uncle Haskell; I had a feeling that she would not have wanted to be like her mother if she could help it. Whatever it was, she had made me happy.

"That's all right, Aunt Cordelia," I said, smiling at her. "I forgive you."

Chapter Three

Christopher and I discovered the secret of Uncle Haskell's nocturnal golfing before the summer was over. About once a month we would see him step buoyantly into the shadowy woods some fine evening, often with a beret set jauntily upon his head, a golf bag without visible clubs slung over his shoulder.

One night we trailed him with what we thought was perfect stealth, keeping clumps of trees and underbrush between us and him, moving slow step by step until the three of us were at the banks of a creek that flowed between the woods and one of the wide fields that Mr. Peters cultivated for our aunt and uncle.

Down at the creek, Uncle Haskell crossed the bridge to the south bank, where the growth of underbrush was heavier, and removed a spade from his golf bag. My heart flopped in sudden terror. A grave, I thought; Uncle Haskell was a monster who dug graves in the moist soil under the bushes, and buried,

Heaven knew what, in the grim depths. Chris took my hand, and I could see the same horror in his face that must have been in mine.

I don't know whether it was our gasps that betrayed us or whether Uncle Haskell had been playing a cat-and-mouse game all along; at any rate when he removed the spade, he stuck it in the ground, leaned upon it a moment, and then chuckled as at some private joke.

"Scat, you little devils," he said pleasantly enough, and we did not wait for further words. We ran breathlessly back through the woods and spent the rest of the evening speculating.

When Uncle Haskell drove into town the next day, presumably for a replenishment of *Le Vieux Corbeau*, we took advantage of his absence to do some further sleuthing.

We got Danny to join us that afternoon, and the three of us raced down to the creek to find what Uncle Haskell had been up to. It didn't take long. The "graves" were quite shallow—Uncle Haskell would not be one to expend a great deal of energy in digging—and we were not long in unearthing what he had buried: empty bottles of *Le Vieux Corbeau*.

It didn't seem sad to us that day. The boys lay on the ground kicking their heels and shrieking, and I joined them, kicking almost as high and shrieking quite as lustily.

During the months of vacation Aunt Cordelia, somewhat against her principles, allowed me to wear my brother's outgrown blue jeans in order to save wear and tear upon my school dresses. I loved that. There was a freedom in blue jeans that delighted me and brought me into closer relationship with Chris and

Danny. Now I could straddle a horse with the same
ease that the boys did when we rode over the country
roads together. The three of us climbed trees and
ran races and helped Mr. Peters cut weeds out of
the corn. Mr. Peters called us his "three boys," and
I couldn't understand how any girl would want a
frilly dress when the joy of blue jeans was available.
And so that afternoon when we discovered Uncle
Haskell's secret, I was able to kick and roll in the grass
with the same abandon enjoyed by Chris and Danny.

But Chris didn't approve of my behavior. He had
always felt a certain responsibility toward me, and
on that afternoon he suddenly stopped laughing and
looked at me sternly.

"You oughtn't to roll on the grass and kick like a
boy, Julie; Laura wouldn't like for you to act like
that."

"Oh, slurp, slurp," I answered airily, but I sat up
all the same, partly because of the reference to Laura,
partly because I had a feeling that Danny agreed
with my brother.

But I had Chris to look after me for only a few
weeks longer that summer. We had told Father about
Uncle Haskell's cemetery of empty bottles, and I think
that our obvious delight in our find set Father to
thinking about the advisability of sending Chris away
to boarding school. Aunt Cordelia reluctantly sec-
onded the proposal, agreeing with Father that Uncle
Haskell was hardly the proper father-figure for a
growing boy. And so Chris had to leave for boarding
school that fall and both of us were desolate for
many weeks. I begged Father to take me home with
him after Chris left, but Aunt Cordelia intervened. I
was too young, she told Father, too undisciplined to

be on my own in town where both Father and Laura were away from home most of the day. I overheard her use the words "strong-willed" and "adventurous" in talking about me. She persuaded Father that I should remain with her until I was ready for high school.

Once again, both Chris and I were manipulated like small puppets in our world of adults. We didn't like it, and we suffered, but the tall ones around us said that we would soon get over our sadness, that we would "adapt" in a matter of weeks.

Poor Chris had only strangers around him, which made his life hard that autumn; I still had Danny and the big horse, Peter the Great, that I claimed as my own. I still had the woods with my cathedral hidden in them and I had Aunt Cordelia, who in her reserved way, was especially kind to me during the days of my sharpest loneliness. And strangely enough, I found that I had a source of comfort in Uncle Haskell. He came up to the house to eat with us a bit oftener that fall, and Aunt Cordelia, true to her mother's upbringing, made these meals very special ones with the best silver and Grandmother's china laid out upon the table. Uncle Haskell was always a gracious guest, gay and serene in his belief that he was doing us an honor in dining with us, but an honor which he was bestowing cheerfully.

There were times when it was good to escape from the quiet austerity of Aunt Cordelia to the gay, never-never land of Uncle Haskell. I was always welcomed to his neat, well-kept living room with its many wall shelves filled about equally with books and bottles. In spite of the fact that I knew the truth wasn't in him, I gave myself up to the delight of listening to accounts of the mythical years when he had roamed the capitals of Europe, loved and courted by the intelligentsia for his wit, for the books he had written (unfortunately all out of print by my day), for his never-failing charm and erudition. He had been quite a man, had Uncle Haskell, and he was about to emerge into a second blooming when his new book appeared, his magnum opus which was carefully kept out of sight in his rooms. It seemed strange, I thought, that I never happened to call on Uncle Haskell when there was a sheet of paper in his typewriter, but I wouldn't have considered it polite to mention the matter. I heard about long-distance telephone calls from his publishers, patient gentlemen it seemed, who urged him to take his time; a magnum opus, they agreed, does not spring into being overnight.

For all my quite justifiable suspicions of his integrity, I liked Uncle Haskell, and he recognized that fact.

"It is no credit either to your discrimination or to your character, my dear child," he told me lightly. "Adam and your sister will have you carted off to a nunnery if you're not very careful to disown me."

It was true that neither Father nor Laura cared for Uncle Haskell. They came out quite often to see me or to take me into town for a holiday in my old home, but on such occasions they did not go back to Uncle Haskell's quarters at all, or if they chanced to meet him, they were pointedly cool. Father was fond of Aunt Cordelia and felt that she had suffered unduly at the hands of an egotistical parasite; Laura mirrored Father's feelings as she had all the years of her life.

How I loved Laura! It was a time of perfect happiness when she came out for the weekend, when we rode together or hiked or swam or skated; most particularly was it perfect for me when we slept together in my room upstairs that had been Mother's when she was a child.

It was Laura who helped me to rid myself of the memory of the gray old woman and the cackling laugh that had frightened me in one of those rooms upstairs; it was also Laura who pointed out the beauty of the changing scene outside my bedroom window, the green and gold and crimson of the woods from spring through autumn, the soft white stillness of winter with the trunks of half a hundred trees standing in penciled darkness against a pale sky.

I would lie close to her, and she would tell me stories or repeat poetry until I went to sleep with the heavenly security of being with someone who was almost Mother.

"You really love me, don't you, Laura?" I asked her.

"I do, indeed, Julie. Very much."

"And we'll always be like this together. You'll never change, will you?"

"Never, Julie," she promised, a little rashly, for she was still quite young.

She did change though. Not much. She still loved me after she was wearing Bill Strohmer's ring, but her eyes were full of dreams, and sometimes she would say, "Let's not talk now, Julie; let's just lie quietly and think for a while."

There was a little change in Laura, but it was still not great enough to alarm me. Sometimes when her eyes were closed, I would prop myself on my elbow to look at the thick lashes against her cheek, at the waves of bright hair that fell back from her forehead. I loved beauty, and I ached with the consciousness

that I would never have the blonde beauty of my
sister. I was dark, more like Father, or as some people
said, like my mother's dour, dark father who had
married a golden flibbertigibbit.

Laura and Bill were married the summer I was ten.
Chris was home for the wedding, very straight and
tall; both he and I were in the wedding party and so
excited over the swarm of activities that I had no
time to brood over the fact that life was again making
a big change for me.

Uncle Haskell sent Laura a silver coffee server
which was charged to Aunt Cordelia's account at one
of the local stores, but he was not able to attend the
wedding. He sent her a note explaining that a deadline set by one of his publishers prevented his being
with his beloved niece on the day of her great happiness. Laura was not crushed.

One very special guest at the wedding was Alicia
Allison, one of Laura's high school teachers, of whom
she was very fond. Miss Allison was a very attractive
woman, I thought, crisp and slender in her coral
linen dress, very youthful looking in spite of her
thirty-eight or forty years and the few lines of glisten-
ing white in her dark hair. Father was especially
attentive to Miss Allison, I noticed; he smiled at me
when I very carefully served her wedding cake and
hurried away to bring her fresh coffee.

I liked Miss Allison, and I thought her name was
lovely. I was beginning to write stories in the privacy
of my room at that time, and for the next several
weeks after Laura's wedding my heroines, most of
them characters who bloomed on paper for several
pages and then faded suddenly, were named "Alicia."

I had a nice note from Laura when she was on her

honeymoon and a line or two from Bill at the bottom
of the sheet. They wanted me to visit them in their
new home, but not for a while, not until all the new
curtains were hung and all the new furniture was in
place. When all that was done, the three of us would
have a wonderful time together. They were both
looking forward to it. Eagerly.

It was a year, however, before I got to visit them.
I missed Laura sharply for a long time, and my day-
dreams were all centered around her, how happy she
would be to see me, how we would lie in bed and
talk until dawn, how she would perhaps say that I
should come to live with her and Bill instead of staying with Aunt Cordelia until I was ready for high
school. Bill, I had rather forgotten. He was a pleasant
young man, friendly and kind, but of no particular
consequence so far as I was concerned. I had something of Uncle Haskell's way of dismissing all persons
for whom I felt no personal need.

Then during the summer of my eleventh year the
three-hundred-mile train ride was behind me, and Bill
was there at the station ready to drive me to their
home and Laura.

She was so terribly changed; she didn't look like
my Laura at all, and for a minute I was dismayed. I
had known that she was going to have a baby; Father
had told me that, but I was not prepared to see her
swollen grotesquely, her bright hair a little dulled,
all the fresh radiance changed to a kind of pallid
weariness. But I was reassured when she kissed me
and joined Bill in laughing at my look of disbelief.

"Don't be shocked, darling; babies do this to their
mamas, you know. Two months from now when you're
Aunt Julie, you'll have a slender sister again—at

least, I hope so," she added with a wry smile at Bill.

"You'll be svelte and the most elegant young mother in town," Bill assured her. "Won't she, Julie?" he added, smiling at me.

Then I kissed her again and followed them around as they showed me all the details of their pretty cottage, told me of the picnic they had planned for the next day, spoke of some girls they had invited over to entertain me on the days when Laura would be busy with some work she was doing for Bill. He was completing his doctorate that summer, and Laura was typing his thesis as well as doing some spots of last minute research and an occasional bit of rewriting. They were both deeply involved in his work, very close and happy, very much like two people welded into a single unit. I didn't quite like it; I felt a nameless fear beginning to grow inside me.

My fear did not become a reality, however, until about ten that evening when Bill ruffled my hair and said, "Well, Laura, hadn't we better let Aunt Julie get her beauty sleep now? She must be a little tired after her long train ride." And Laura said, "Yes, darling, come along. I'll show you the room you're to have."

She would show me the room *I* was to have, not the one *we* would share. There was a single bed in that room with a blue dust ruffle around it and a lacy white spread on top. It was a very pretty room and a pretty bed, but it was not a room to be shared by two sisters, not a bed where they could lie close together, where they could talk girl-talk until their eyes grew heavy and they drifted off to sleep, almost as secure as in the days when a mother had been alive.

Laura wouldn't look at me. I tried to force her to

look into my eyes. If she would do that, I knew she would see there my agony and she would say, "Yes, Julie, I'm going to stay here with you." That Bill doesn't much matter. But she wouldn't look at me; she kept chattering about the paper they had picked out with me in mind, about how I could sleep as long as I pleased the next morning, and would I like for her to make blueberry muffins for our breakfast. But she wouldn't look at me, and when she kissed me good-night, there was still the pretense that she didn't know I was sick with disappointment.

I cried on the white pillow that night and, switching on the bedside lamp, I was impressed by the sad stain my tears had made. Then I thought how Laura would never notice and would send the slip out to some laundry and impersonal hands would wash away the marks of grief, never knowing, never caring that part of a little girl had died with those tears. Then I cried again at that thought, and I felt the great loneliness I had felt that day of Mother's funeral. But this time my loneliness was mixed with resentment and an unreasoning jealousy.

Things were better the next morning. Both Laura and Bill were very gay and obviously determined to see that I was happy. We ate in the sunny kitchen from the gay breakfast service that Alicia Allison had given Laura for a wedding gift, and breakfast was delicious: fruit and muffins, bacon, strawberry preserves, and coffee blended with hot milk. Bill teased me a little, wondering if I had blacked any more little boys' eyes for the reason that I had blacked Danny's; Laura thought that my new blue robe was very becoming, and she and Bill agreed over my head that I was really growing up to be a very pretty girl.

Everything was delightful and it should have remained that way except that the dark streak within me refused to be propitiated.

When Bill had gone off to the university and Laura and I had finished the dishes, she gave me a new book, bought especially for me, and suggested that I read while she looked up some references that Bill needed for his thesis. It was then that I wondered, not in so many words, but quite pointedly, if Bill had not sufficient academic aptitude to do his own research.

That brought the first flare to my sister's eyes and she assured me of Bill's brilliance and of her own gratitude that she was able in a small way to help him in an effort that meant so much to both of them. She said something about the fact that Father had considered Bill the ablest student he had known in years, and seeing that she was angry already, I dug my claws in deeper and told her that Uncle Haskell said that Father was a man of "middle class values."

Then she really did throw out sparks. "You tell Uncle Haskell," she said angrily, "that if by 'middle class values' he means a sense of integrity, a willingness to contribute to society rather than to be a leech, then Father is, indeed, a man of 'middle class values.' Uncle Haskell should talk of values—if he has any at all, they are of the shoddiest sort. I think it's high time," she added furiously, "that Father marries Alicia and gets you away from Uncle Haskell's influence."

It had never occurred to me that there was a remote possibility of Father's marrying Alicia. Father was married to Mother and that was the way things were and should always be, world without end, and I thought that Laura should be heartily ashamed of herself for the remark she had just made.

"If Father marries Alicia—if Father marries any woman in this world, I'll never go home again; never, as long as I live. I should think that you would love Mother enough to feel that way too," I added accusingly.

If I had known how tired and unwell Laura was feeling at that time, I surely would have been kinder. But I had no interest in anyone's feelings save my own, and for the first time, I deliberately tried to hurt the feelings of the person I loved above all others.

Laura grew almost hysterical with tears and anger as she defended her own love for Mother and her wish to see Father with a companion of whom Mother would have approved. "I don't know what has happened to you, Julie," she sobbed, wiping her eyes. "You have always been such a darling child. What has got into you?"

I was miserable by that time, ashamed and sorry. "I don't know," I wailed, "unless it's because I'm standing where the brook and river meet."

Then Laura said, "Oh, good Heavens," in a tone that suggested I had said something completely idiotic, and she laughed at the same time she was crying in such a way that I was at first deeply offended and then frightened. It was an unhappy morning.

We smoothed each other's feelings, of course, and the visit was not quite spoiled. But it was a disappointment, a dreary, heartbreaking disappointment, and when we kissed one another good-bye the morning I left, we were both heavy with the certainty that we had lost something precious.

Bill took me to the station that morning, a very grave young man and unusually kind. He explained that if Laura had seemed a little sharp, a little unlike herself, it was because she was not well, that she was nervous and perhaps a little anxious in her first pregnancy. He told me that she loved me very much, that she was going to name the baby "Julie" if it was a girl, that the three of us would back Aunt Cordelia into a corner and persuade her that the French "Julie" was quite as legal as the Roman "Julia." There wasn't a word about my share of the blame for which I had no excuse except a childish jealousy. My sense of guilt was very deep when I boarded the train for my journey home.

I sat beside a window on the green mohair seat and stared out at the countryside, all but lost in a gray mist of rain. I thought of Laura having a baby, and I wondered if it hurt dreadfully and considered the possibility that she might die. And how, I thought, could I live the rest of my life remembering how she had tried to make me happy in all the little ways she could, and how I had repaid her with snide and cruel remarks that had possibly destroyed all the love she had felt for me. Finally I covered my face with my hands and shook with the misery pent up inside me.

A gray-haired, blue-uniformed conductor had looked at me kindly when he took my ticket, and after a while he came back, bringing me a chocolate bar bulging with almonds. He sat down in the seat beside me when I thanked him tearfully, and he patted my shoulder.

"Maybe it would help to talk about it," he said gently. "I've raised five little girls to womanhood; like as not I'll be able to understand."

To my surprise, I told him all about it, this stranger whom I would probably never see again. I had to tell someone, and I knew that it would shame me terribly to tell either Father or Aunt Cordelia. And so I talked and talked, sometimes between sobs, and although it didnt bring me peace of mind, it somehow helped for me to put my guilt feelings into words.

The conductor nodded often during my story and when I was through, he was silent for a long time. He pursed his lips thoughtfully and tapped the fingers of his left hand against the arm of the seat.

Finally he spoke, almost as if to himself. "It happens the world over—we love ourselves more than we do the one we say we love. We all want to be Number One; we've got to be Number One or nothing! We can't see that we could make ourselves loved and needed in the Number Two, or Three, or Four spot. No sir, we've got to be Number One, and if we can't make it, we'll rip and tear at the loved one till we've ruined every smidgin of love that was ever there." He sighed. "I don't know what to tell you, little lady."

He had to leave me then to go about his duties, and he didn't return to my seat until it was almost time for the train to pull into the station where Father would be waiting for me. Then he leaned down and spoke to me almost in a whisper. "I believe that, was I you, I'd try growing up a little and giving some thought about what I could do for my big sister from the Number Three or Four spot."

The last days of that summer were troubled ones for me. I wondered if I had ripped and torn at Laura as the conductor had said people did, the world over, if I had destroyed all her love for me because of my anger at being somewhere other than in the "Number

One Spot." I recalled all the brattish things I had said, though I wanted to forget them. The little Cathedral of Four Silver Birches became my hideaway during those troubled days, and the tears I shed were those of the true penitent.

Aunt Cordelia noticed my preoccupation, and she was unusually kind. "Laura is young and healthy and under good medical care, Julia. I don't think that we need to be fearful. In a few weeks she will be as happy as your mother used to be after each of you was born."

I nodded, but the dreariness inside me was undiminished. Even when Father called us early one morning in September to tell us that Laura and Bill had a little daughter, that Laura was well and happy, that the baby was healthy and beautiful—even then, I crawled off to my cathedral and wept because I didn't believe that Laura could ever really love me again.

A new year of school had begun and each day Aunt Cordelia and I marched off to the white schoolhouse, sometimes joined by Danny and Carlotta, all of us employing our diaphragms in deep breathing and obediently fixing our thoughts upon the beauty of September skies and the glory of wild asters and goldenrod—sometimes with sly grins at one another. Once again I lost my identity as Aunt Cordelia's niece, put my mind upon the tasks she set for me, avoided Aggie Kilpin, became a devoted friend and then an avowed enemy of Carlotta Berry. But this year was different; I missed Chris sharply when I looked at the empty seat beside Danny, and I grieved, even as I learned to find the area and circumference of a circle, for my big sister's love which I was sure that I had lost forever.

Another telephone call came on the sixth of September. I shall never forget the date for it was the day of my return to happiness. Aunt Cordelia answered the telephone. I heard her address someone as "William"— that would be Bill, of course—heard her ask about Laura and the baby, heard her say thoughtfully that yes, she thought it could be arranged; no, the schoolwork could be made up easily; yes, she felt that it would be a good thing for both girls. Then she called me to the telephone and Bill's voice, now grown very dear to me, told me that the baby's name was "Julie," that Laura was home from the hospital, that he had wanted to hire a woman to help her with the baby, but that Laura had said no, she wanted her sister with her for the next few days. He asked me if I would come, and I began to cry and told him between hiccoughs that, yes, I would be there.

Aunt Cordelia found one of my old dolls that evening, and she showed me how to protect an infant's head and back; she told me what an extra pillow could mean in a new mother's chair and how a flower on a luncheon tray could make a plain bowl of soup something of a treat for a convalescent.

When I went to my room that night the world was a better and brighter place, and I was controlled by a new discipline which I imposed sternly upon myself.

"Bill is in the Number One Spot, and don't forget it, Julie Trelling. And the baby is in the Number Two Spot." I hesitated at that point, and then drew the haircloth shirt a little tighter. Father was in the

Number Three Spot, one had just as well admit it. But when I thought of Chris preceding me as Number Four, I balked. Chris could share that place, I supposed, but that was all. There was a limit to my humility.

When I burrowed down between my white sheets that night, I breathed deeply of happiness. I wished that I could tell the old conductor how wise I had grown; I thought of how much more than an almond chocolate bar he had given me.

Chapter Four

My twelfth year, we supposed, would be my last one
with Aunt Cordelia, since I would be entering high
school the next year and be going into town to live
with Father; therefore Aunt Cordelia agreed that I
might have a birthday party that spring and the talk
among the girls at school centered for a period of
several weeks upon the social event of the season.
Word of it got to Aggie Kilpin, who still sat in the
center of a wide circle of peasants during the noon
hour; Aggie gleefully told me that yes, kid, she would
be coming to my party too. I didn't think she would.

Alicia Allison sent me a box of tiny pink notes and
matching envelopes on which I could write, "Miss
Julie Trelling requests the pleasure," and so on. I
spent a happy and satisfying hour in preparing these
notes and addressing each tiny envelope. Aunt Cordelia had said, "Boys and girls, or just girls?" when
I had suggested the party, and I had decided in favor
of just girls, including some of the girls from town.

Since she hadn't demurred at the exclusion of boys, I rather hoped that she would not notice one other omission. She did, of course. Ruffling through the little pile of envelopes, she said quietly, "Julia, you have forgotten to include Agnes."

"Oh, Aunt Cordelia, I can't. I simply can't have Aggie. She would spoil the whole party. You know that."

"She knows about your party, Julia, and it has been something she's looked forward to for weeks. You can't do this to another child; it would be too cruel."

"I can't invite her. I simply can't have the town girls thinking that she is my friend. I'm sorry for Aggie, awfully sorry, but let's face it, Aunt Cordelia: Aggie smells."

Aunt Cordelia sighed. "Julia, that child has been in my classroom since she was five; that means she's been there almost ten years, and she has stood at my desk, learning nothing, but giving off a more unbearable stench each year. I know Agnes very well; I know that she's smelly as you say, but I also know that if you stab her, she feels pain. I can't encourage cruelty on your part."

I shook my head. "I'd rather not have a party if I have to ask her," I said shortly.

"That's up to you, Julia; think it over," Aunt Cordelia answered.

I made my decision. The little pink envelopes went into the wastebasket, and I had to tell all the girls at school that there would be no party. There was general indignation directed toward Aunt Cordelia, indignation coming from my closest friends, from some of their mothers, even from Aggie, who muttered that

Miss Cordelia was mean to Julie, never once suspecting that she herself was the cause of all our broken plans.

Aunt Cordelia maintained her usual calm. No one of us was fool enough to believe that she would change her mind though the whole school should rise in mutiny. Her only nod to our disappointment was a casual remark that, although the party had been cancelled, there would be birthday cake for everyone, a remark that delighted the boys, who had not been especially pained at the disappointment of the girls in the first place.

Father never interfered with Aunt Cordelia's disciplinary measures, but I think that he felt a little sorry for me at this time. He came out and took me for a long drive the night before my birthday, and he brought me a silver pen and a quire of good white paper in a leather box, material for the stories I wanted to write. Alicia sent me a gift too, a beautifully bound volume of Edna St. Vincent Millay's poems. In a little note Alicia said, "There is something about you, Julie, that reminds me of Millay's early poems; read them now and save the darker ones for later years." She had placed her note in the book so that it opened to the lines:

"God, I can push the grass apart
And lay my finger on Your heart!"

And turning a few pages, I found lines that mirrored an ache and longing I had so often felt when the beauty around my woods cathedral was too intense, when the need to grasp and keep loveliness left me with a sense of desolate frustration.

"Thy winds, thy wide gray skies!
Thy mists that roll and rise!
Thy woods, this autumn day, that ache and sag
And all but cry with color! That gaunt crag
To crush! To lift the lean of that black bluff!
World, world, I cannot get thee close enough!"

When I was through, my eyes were wet and I
loved not only Millay but Alicia and Laura and Aunt
Cordelia—almost everyone in the world except poor
little Aggie Kilpin.

Compassion was not yet aroused within me, and
the better nature that loved poetry and beauty was
completely overshadowed the day of my twelfth birthday. Aunt Cordelia drove her car to school that
morning because she was taking the two huge angel-
food cakes that she had baked and iced the night
before. I was invited to cut the cakes at noon and
after sliding each piece on a napkin, to place my
birthday offering on each pupil's desk. It was a poor
substitute for a party, and most of the girls felt as
downcast and low spirited that noon as I did.

But not Aggie. She grinned in delight when I
placed the cake before her, and she clambered out
of her seat when she saw the rest of us preparing to
go outside.

"I won't be queen today, kid," she garbled eagerly.
"I'm goin' to set by you 'cause it's your birthday. I'm
goin' to be your best friend."

And then I did it, a thing one does not forget. I
turned on an innocent human being in fury, and I
threw Aggie's love for me back into her simple, uncomprehending face.

"Don't you dare follow me, Aggie; don't you dare
come near me," I told her, and I didn't care in the

least what measures of discipline Aunt Cordelia might think up for me. I flashed a hostile look toward her as I strode past her desk, and I noticed that she looked quite tired and a little drawn. She said nothing to me, but she held out her hand to Aggie.

"Would you like to go with the little children and me, Agnes? We're going out to the woods and get a bunch of wild flowers for Julia's birthday."

Aggie seemed to be afraid of me after that. She would grin timidly at me and nod her head as if encouraging me to be kind. Sometimes in shame, I returned her smile, but it was always a weak thing, and Aggie was never reassured. I did not read Edna St. Vincent Millay's poems during those last few weeks of school; belatedly, I had a miserable feeling that the gentle young poet would not have liked me.

It was a hot, dry summer that year, and in early August, when the heat seemed almost unbearable, we heard that Agnes Kilpin was very ill with a fever resulting from the infection of a cut foot for which she had received no medical attention. Aunt Cordelia immediately drove up to the Kilpins', taking ice and cool fruit drinks with her. That evening she told me something of the condition in which she had found Aggie and of the futility of trying to help her.

"I wanted to bathe the poor child and put clean sheets on her bed, but Mrs. Kilpin wouldn't allow me to touch her—said she wasn't going to have her girl catch pneumonia by having a bath." Aunt Cordelia closed her eyes briefly in exasperation. "Afraid of pneumonia, but not of filth and the agony of heat and fever. I wanted to tie that woman up outside the room and see to it that Agnes was cared for properly —for just once in her life."

A few days later on a hot Sunday when tempers

were shorter than usual, Aunt Cordelia and I had
one of our not infrequent clashes. She had given my
room a quick inspection after church that morning,
and had found its condition unsatisfactory.

"You will put your books and clothing in their
proper places, Julia, and you will dust the room, including—especially including—the windowsills, which
I find absolutely white with dust. And understand
this, Julia: no lady has a right to that title unless she
is not only clean of body and clothing, but is equally
clean in her surroundings. Never let it be said that
you have grown up in my home and have been so
remiss as to throw your discarded underclothing under
the bed—which is exactly where I found yours just
now."

Her wrath was formidable; mine was rather intense too, for I felt that I might have been instructed
to clean my room with considerably less sermonizing.
Our clash was brief and bitter, and Aunt Cordelia
was the victor. I spent the next hour converting the
energy of rage into a zest for cleaning which resulted
in an immaculate state that would have satisfied any
top-sergeant.

Aunt Cordelia inspected my work and nodded ap-
provingly. "I should think now that after a shower
and a brief apology for your impertinence you might
feel very much better, Julia."

"I am very sorry that I was impertinent, Aunt
Cordelia," I managed to say, and then fled for the
bathroom and a shower. I wished as I stood under
the cooling, cleansing flood of water that I were as
fortunate as Uncle Haskell, living apart in the old
carriage house, working on a magnum opus and communicating with Aunt Cordelia only infrequently.

That was the afternoon that Carlotta Berry called, asking me to go driving with her. To receive an invitation to go driving with Lottie that summer was a coveted honor. Being an only child of unusually indulgent parents, Lottie had a great deal more in the way of clothes and expensive toys than most of us, and for her birthday that year she had received a gift that was the envy of all her classmates. The gift was a pony, a snowy, dainty-hoofed little creature, a wonderful gift in itself, but this one was harnessed to a wicker and patent leather cart. Carlotta had power in the possession of that pony cart: those who pleased her might share it, but there were no rides for those who did not.

I supposed no favors would be granted me that afternoon, but Aunt Cordelia was a much fairer person than I sometimes believed her to be.

"I see no reason why you shouldn't go," she said pleasantly. "You have fulfilled your duties and are entitled to some recreation."

"I can go!" I told Lottie joyfully, and when she arrived, cool and pretty in blue and white organdy, Aunt Cordelia looked at me thoughtfully and suggested that I might wear the dress from Laura's wardrobe which she had altered to fit me, a fine white linen embroidered with tiny wreaths of rosy flowers and tied with a gay sash. It was plain that Aunt Cordelia wanted me to look no less well-dressed than the darling of the Berry household.

Our gladiolas were in full bloom that week and while I dressed, Aunt Cordelia cut a great armful of the bright flowers and then sat in the porch swing waiting for Carlotta and me to come downstairs.

"Since you're going to be driving all around the

neighborhood, I think it would be nice of you girls to take this bouquet to Agnes. You won't mind doing that, will you?" she asked.

Aunt Cordelia was too much the voice of authority for either Carlotta or me to resist her suggestion. We didn't want to think of Aggie, much less to visit her, but a sense of decency prodded by the determination which we knew was back of my aunt's quiet suggestion, led us to accept the errand.

"Isn't it just like her?" Carlotta sputtered when we were out of hearing. "She spoils your party on account of Aggie, and now, she spoils our afternoon by making us stop at the dirty Kilpins'. Sometimes I can't *stand* Miss Cordelia; I mean it—I just can't *stand* her."

I had been annoyed too, but at that speech I turned loyal niece and remarked that if Lottie didn't like my aunt, she might well have invited someone other than a relative of Aunt Cordelia's to go riding with her, and Lottie replied that since the pony and cart were hers, she might rescind her invitation.

I wanted the ride enough to tolerate Carlotta's airs. Both of us were conscious that we made a pretty picture on the country road, our gay dresses and the bright flowers filling the little cart with color, Lottie's blonde hair and my black shining as brightly as the pony's silver coat. Uncle Haskell took off his hat and made us a sweeping bow when we met him driving home from town, and a mile or so farther on, Danny Trevort and Jimmy Ferris chased us on their bicycles, scorning our elegance although we were pretty sure that they secretly envied us.

"O, ki-tinka, ka-tonka," they shrilled in pained mockery. Then, riding close to the cart and holding on to the sides, they gave us the benefit of their supreme contempt. "Slurp, slurp," they added as if the sight of us was a little more than either of them could bear.

Their behavior bothered me a little. Danny was still as close to me as in the days when he and Chris and I rode and swam and skated together. Danny was often at Aunt Cordelia's, and I was just as often at his home where gentle Mrs. Trevort always made me welcome. Now, in the presence of Carlotta and Jimmy, he was scornful of me, and I found myself acting as haughtily toward him as if we were foes of long standing.

There is something wrong with this world, I thought. And then, a few minutes later, I found a world in which there was a greater wrong than I had ever known.

Carlotta refused to go inside when we reached the Kilpin house.

"I don't have to mind Miss Cordelia while it's summer vacation, Julie," she said, and I had to respect her point of view. "I guess you'll just have to take the flowers in yourself—since you can't help being her niece." She glanced back down the road, obviously hoping the boys would soon appear again.

I climbed out of the elegant cart and crossed the road in some trepidation. I had heard stories of the Kilpins; they were trash, and vicious trash at that. The cluttered dooryard and the sagging front steps added to the ominous look of the place; I rather hoped that no one would hear my light knock on the half-open screen door.

But Mrs. Kilpin had seen my approach, and she came to the door as soon as I knocked. She was a withered, bent woman with a narrow strip of forehead wrinkling above close-set, sullen eyes. She motioned me to come in, but she didn't speak; when I offered her the flowers and told her they were for Aggie, she nodded toward a table where I laid them, pretty sure that they wouldn't be touched until they were thrown away.

Aggie was lying on a bed in the corner of the room. It was a filthy bed, sheetless and sagging in the middle, and Aggie rolled restlessly upon it, her mouth parched with fever and her eyes glazed and unseeing. The heat, the stench, and the closeness of death made the place so unbearable that I wanted nothing so much as to break away and run from it. Somehow, however, I managed to walk closer to the bed and speak to the girl who lay there.

I really think that I half expected to see Aggie grin again, to hear her call me "Kid" and declare that we were friends. But Aggie was another person that day; she was a part of the dignity of a solemn drama, no longer the phony "queen" seated in the center of a mocking circle of her subjects. Aggie was as indifferent to my presence as if I'd been one of the houseflies crawling along the edge of a spoon that lay on the table beside a bottle of medicine.

I was awed and unsure of what I should do. "Is she going to get well?" I finally whispered to the shadowy woman who stood beside me.

"No, she ain't a-goin' to git well. She's a-goin' to die," the woman said without emotion.

"I'm sorry," I said, and Mrs. Kilpin answered in the same dead voice.

"No, you ain't. You ain't sorry. Nobody's sorry that my girl's a-goin' to die. Not even her pa's sorry. Nobody."

I couldn't answer that. "I guess I must go, Mrs. Kilpin," I said miserably. "I guess I'll have to go."

"Yes, you go," she said, and I saw her eyes studying me from head to foot. "Them clothes is too fine for this place. You go 'long."

I turned toward the bed with agony in my throat. If I could have kept Aggie from dying by ignoring the stench and the ugliness, it would have been such an easy thing to do; it would have been a privilege to put my cheek next to hers and to tell her that yes, I was her friend. But Aggie would not look at me, and her mother's look held only sullen hatred for me.

"I know that sometimes I've been mean to Aggie. I'm sorry, Mrs. Kilpin; I wish that you'd believe me. I'm really sorry."

"I said that you'd best be gittin' on," Mrs. Kilpin said, without looking at me. She pointed toward the door.

When I was out of the house, I ran to the cart where Carlotta was waiting. "Hurry, Julie," she said, her doll-like face pink with anticipation. "We're going to go north at the corner. The boys just went that way, and I almost know they're hiding to surprise us. We won't even speak to them," she added, the instincts of the born coquette asserting themselves more strongly by the minute.

"Take me home, Lottie," I said desperately, as I climbed into the seat beside her. "Please. Just take me home—then you can do whatever you like."

"Don't be silly, Julie. For goodness sake, was it *that* bad? I didn't know you liked Aggie so much."

"Will you take me home?" I asked her once again, my voice sharp because of the tumult inside me.

"No, I won't. Your old aunt had to spoil things by

making us come up here. My mother didn't say that
I had to come and see Aggie, but I just brought you
up here because I supposed that Miss Cordelia would
have a fit if I didn't. Now, I'm going to go wherever
I please, and I just don't please to take you home."

It wasn't the first time we had quarreled. Lottie
and I were at swords' points as often as we were
bound together in friendship. And beside the fact
that our friendship was not very deep, the day was
ghastly hot and beyond the discomfort of heat I
was sickened by the glimpse I'd had of "something
terribly wrong in this world." I jumped from the seat
into the dusty road.

"Go right ahead," I told her. "I'll walk."

"Very well, Miss Trelling," Carlotta said loftily, and
off she drove, her pony and cart, her blonde curls and
organdy dress as beautiful as a picture.

There were two miles before me, and I was already
tired. The thick yellow dust felt hot through my thin
slippers, and the half-burned weeds stung when they
swished about my bare ankles. It would have been
a long and wretched walk if Danny hadn't rescued
me, but he did, and there wasn't a trace of the taunts
he had yelled at Carlotta and me hardly a half hour
earlier.

"What's the matter, Julie?" he asked as he stopped
his bicycle at my side. "What did Lottie do to you?"

"Nothing. She just won't take me home." I looked
at Danny bleakly. "I think Aggie is going to die,
Danny, and her mother almost hates me. I can't ride
around the country in a pony cart after I've seen
Aggie and her mother."

Danny looked down at the ground. Somehow the

subject of death embarrassed us both. I wondered about it later.

I rode for the remainder of the two miles home on the handlebars of Danny's bicycle. We didn't talk much, and Aunt Cordelia didn't say much either when I told her briefly what had happened. Some grease from the spokes of a wheel had soiled my white dress, but she didn't scold; she made cold lemonade for Danny and me and the three of us sat together on the wide porch, all of us grave and thoughtful.

Mrs. Kilpin had been right; we heard of Aggie's death the next morning, and Aunt Cordelia again drove up to the bare, wretched home where she and Mrs. Trevort and Mrs. Peters got Aggie ready for a decent burial.

The three women looked pale and tired when they came back from the Kilpins that night. Aunt Cordelia and I sat together in the high-ceilinged library where a cross-current of air made the room cool and pleasant.

"She's clean, at last, poor little creature." Aunt Cordelia shuddered involuntarily when she spoke. "I washed her hair. It was a task the like of which I hope never to have to do again. But do you know, Julia, the child had pretty hair. When it was clean I was able to press two big waves in it above her forehead, and when it dried it was a deep brown color with bright lights in it."

Aggie's hair clean. Not only clean, but pretty. It seemed impossible, but I knew that it was true or Aunt Cordelia would not have said so. I wished that Aggie could have known. It seemed such a terrible waste—ugliness all one's life, and something pretty discovered only after one was dead.

I had never attended a funeral; Aunt Cordelia had always excused me from going with her for one reason or another. But four of us, Elsie Devers, Margaret Moore, Carlotta and I, were pressed into attending Aggie's funeral. We carried big armfuls of flowers and followed Aggie's casket to the altar of the little country church.

When I looked at Aggie lying in her coffin that afternoon, I was filled with wonder as I saw that she was gently, almost gracefully pretty in death. She was clean, so beautifully clean in the soft ivory-colored dress that my aunt and other neighbors had bought for her, a dress that would have sent Aggie into ecstacies if she could have had it while she lived. I noticed that her hair was, indeed, bright with copper lights in it, lights that sparkled when the afternoon sunlight, channeled in through the church windows, touched Aggie's head and face. It had been the filth and the stench and the silly grimaces, the garbled speech and the stupid responses that had made Aggie revolting. And now she was pretty.

But it was a prettiness touched with a cold aloofness that reproached and tormented me. I knew with a terrible certainty that I might beg her forgiveness until I was exhausted, that I might kneel before her as we had done in mockery when we first made her queen of the lunch hour, and that she would remain as coldly indifferent to me as I had once been to her.

There was a poem of Sara Teasdale's which I had heard Aunt Cordelia read many times. It hadn't meant much to me until that afternoon when, I found to my surprise, that I was able to recall every word of it. I whispered the lines to myself:

"When I am dead and over me bright April
Shakes out her rain-drenched hair,
Though you should lean above me broken-hearted
I shall not care.

I shall have peace, as lofty trees are peaceful
When rain bends down the bough;
And I shall be more silent and cold-hearted
Than you are now."

When we walked home after the funeral, Carlotta
said, "You were saying poetry to yourself in the
church, Julie. I think that's very bad manners, with
poor Aggie lying there dead—and all that."

At twilight that evening I wandered out to the
carriage house, where Uncle Haskell sat on his porch
enjoying the light breeze that stirred the leaves of
our surrounding wooded acres. He laughed lightly as
I seated myself on the steps at his feet.

"Your face, my treasure, has a funereal aspect this
evening. Are you responding to our popular stereo-
type—the proper mourner who must tense his mus-
cles for the correct number of days before he can
cheerfully thank Heaven that it was the other fellow
and not he, who had succumbed?"

I didn't answer immediately. Sometimes Uncle Haskell seemed like a bad-mannered child, someone who
deserved to be ignored.

"Do you know what it means to feel guilty, Uncle
Haskell?" I asked after a minute.

"No. I thank whatever gods may be that no such
emotion has ever disrupted my equanimity." He toyed
for a while with the pipe which he always carried but

never smoked. "Now, why should you feel guilty, my little Julie? You know very well that if this Kilpin girl could approach you again, as moronic and distasteful as she was a month ago, that you'd feel the same revulsion for her. You couldn't help it."

He was right, of course. I thought how awkward it would be to have to say, "Oh, Aggie you were so nice when you were dead, and now here you are—the same old mess again." That wouldn't do, naturally; one couldn't say *that*, even to Aggie.

Uncle Haskell was speaking again. "Hadn't you rather thank Heaven that she has escaped what life had to offer her? And isn't it a blessing that society escaped a multiplication of her kind? Come, Julie, death may be the great equalizer; let's not give in to the hypocrisy that it is the great glorifier."

We sat in silence after that, and I listened to the sounds of night around us. Uncle Haskell's words beat in upon me as I sat there; I knew that he expressed something that was true, but I knew as well that he was missing something. In Aggie's life and death there was something more than a distasteful little unfortunate's few barren years and her fever-driven death. But what it was I could not put into words; it was strange that I should have sought out a cynic such as Uncle Haskell with the hope of finding an answer.

Finally I rose, the need for action of some sort strong within me. "I think I'll saddle Peter the Great and ride for a while," I said.

Then, for some reason, I suddenly felt very sorry for Uncle Haskell. Obeying an impulse which I did not understand, I mounted the five steps up to the porch, and standing beside his chair, I bent and kissed him on his forehead. It was the first time in my life that I had ever done anything of the kind.

He didn't move. He muttered, "Don't ride too far," and that was all. I ran out to the barn, saddled the big old horse who was much gentler than his namesake, and rode away through the woods, pondering for the first time over the mysteries of life and death.

Uncle Haskell's light was on when I returned, and I could see that he was working at his typewriter. That was unusual. His writings never seemed to reach his typewriter; one supposed, innocently at first and then in mocking derision, that his magnum opus was being done in longhand.

I slept rather late the next morning and when I opened my eyes, I saw the folded white paper which had been slipped underneath my door. I jumped out of bed to pick it up and then propped myself comfortably against the pillows in order to enjoy whatever it was that I was about to read.

The letter read as follows:

Dear Julie:

What you were seeking tonight was a good, gray uncle, full of wisdom, and you came to an uncle who is neither good nor gray nor very wise.

I am annoyed with you, my sweet. I do not like stepping out of character even for a little niece who kisses me good-night, and by that token, makes a vapid old fool of me. But I'll be for a few minutes your good, gray uncle, full of wisdom. I'll say to my sad-faced little Julie: Guilt feelings will do nothing for either you or the Kilpin child. But your compassion as you grow into womanhood may well become immortality for the girl you call "Aggie."

Uncle Haskell

I read his letter several times and then secreted it in the little leather box where I hid other treasures. Hopefully, I half expected to find a changed Uncle Haskell that morning, a man who had given up lying and drinking and had awakened to his responsibilities to society. But he hadn't changed; he did not show by a single glance that he remembered the note he had written to me.

Chapter Five

Uncle Haskell had mentioned the name of Jonathan Eltwing once or twice; Mrs. Peters had also spoken of him in a mysterious way as if she didn't want Aunt Cordelia to overhear her. Once I had grown bold enough to say quite casually, "Do you know a man named Jonathan Eltwing, Aunt Cordelia?"

She hadn't blinked an eye. She said very smoothly, "I knew him a number of years ago, Julia. Why do you ask?"

I was embarrassed then and ill at ease. "I just wondered," I said.

"Then it was an idle question, wasn't it?"

"Yes, ma'am," I answered and resolved never to get myself out on such a limb again.

But when I went to help Laura out the fall little Julie was born, I remembered to ask her what she knew about this character, Jonathan Eltwing. Mother had long ago told Laura all about the man who, she suspected, had once been Aunt Cordelia's sweetheart.

I listened, agog with interest, as Laura repeated the story to me.

Jonathan Eltwing was about Aunt Cordelia's age, which meant that he must have been eighteen the fall she commenced teaching in the country school. She was still teaching in the same school thirty-five years later, when Chris and I with all the others sat at the wooden desks and watched her firm hand write out instructions and examples on the blackboard.

He had come to school that fall, this awkward, earnest boy who towered above the young teacher, and he confided in her the hope that some day he might be able to go to college, although the hope was dim for he had neither money nor the prerequisite high school training. The father of the Eltwing children had little use for higher learning, and was unwilling either to pay for their schooling or to allow himself to be deprived of the benefits of their labor on his farm. However, he had made one foolish mistake: he had married a woman who had a hunger for learning, and every one of their six children was born with her intelligence and was later stimulated by her to seek an education. Jonathan was the first; encouraged by his mother and Aunt Cordelia, he broke with his father and started the climb which was to lead to the finest universities of the country and to the highest academic honors. The other five, one by one, followed him.

Aunt Cordelia had been immediately fired by anger against the father and sympathy for the son. She had family problems of her own, even at eighteen, but she turned them aside that winter and gave herself up fully to the project of getting Jonathan Eltwing ready for his college entrance examinations.

She had only a high school education herself, but she had been an excellent student, and she was a natural teacher. She carried loads of her own books to school, and she and young Eltwing mapped out a course of study that would have overwhelmed two youngsters of less enthusiasm and determination.

It was soon apparent to Aunt Cordelia that she had excellent material with which to work. Jonathan Eltwing had high intelligence and a motivation that drove him to attack with fury the piles of work she laid out for him. She was delighted when he soon overtook her in mathematics and the natural sciences; she guided his reading in history, in American and English literature, and in spite of an occasional groan from him, she made him learn a little Latin and considerable English grammar and rhetoric.

They worked together early of a morning before school, and then during the day while Aunt Cordelia taught younger pupils, Jonathan Eltwing sat at a desk in the back of the room and labored at the pile of work his young teacher had assigned to him. In the late afternoon, following the dismissal of the other children, they worked again, sometimes until the winter twilight drove them home.

Of course, tongues began to wag in hopeful suspicion that youthful immorality was afoot in the small schoolhouse, and one evening Aunt Cordelia had word that the directors of the school planned to visit her the following morning.

My grandfather seems to have had perfect confidence in his daughter and pride in what she was doing for Jonathan Eltwing. Grim, tight-lipped old Amos Bishop went with Aunt Cordelia to school that morning, and while she and Jonathan stood on either side

of him, gave the school fathers a stern dressing-down.
However, after that scene, Aunt Cordelia always kept
my mother, a child of eight or ten, with her after
school hours. Laura told me the story of how Mother
would sit reading in the back of the room from four
until five or later, a patient little chaperone guarding
the good name of her sister.

Whether the two had fallen in love that winter, no
one ever quite knew. Laura said that Mother thought
they did. She remembered looks that passed between
them, and clasped hands that were quickly unclasped;
she remembered too, that on the night before Jonathan left for college she had seen two shadowy figures
standing close together in the dusky woods beyond
her window. She remembered that many letters came
for a while, that finally they came much more rarely,
that Aunt Cordelia became less pretty. with a tight-
ened mouth and a stiffer air. She never had another
"beau" and by the time she was twenty, people were
speaking of her as "the old-maid school teacher."

Jonathan Eltwing took advanced degrees, performed brilliantly in the various universities he attended, became an authority on Russian literature,
and married a delicate girl with large, brilliant eyes
and a passion for music.

Through the years he had never returned to the
community until the autumn which I remember. His
mother had joined him as soon as he was able to support her; the father had died, never seeing or even
asking about his oldest son until a few days before
his death when he had inquired of a neighbor if the
man knew what "this Phi Beta Kappa business was
all about." He had read in the local paper that it was
something that had happened to Jonathan.

One day in the fall of my twelfth year, Father called Aunt Cordelia, and I remember that her face flushed and then grew pale as she stood at the old-fashioned telephone anchored against the dining room wall. I heard her say, "Why, of course, Adam; I'd like very much to see Jonathan again and to meet Mrs. Eltwing. Why don't you bring them out Saturday, say, at three in the afternoon?"

She was quite calm and matter-of-fact when she turned away from the telephone. "Your father tells me that Dr. Jonathan Eltwing is buying the old Merridan place and is moving out here for the winter while he finishes his latest book." She corrected the height of a window shade and ran her finger across the sill at which gesture I trembled, but she smiled at me in a very friendly way. "You really are becoming very careful, Julia; your dusting is much more thorough than it used to be."

I decided to try once again. "Who is Dr. Jonathan Eltwing, Aunt Cordelia?" I asked, betting to myself that she would never get into the romantic angle involving the distinguished professor.

She didn't. She raised her brows ever so slightly and adjusted another shade. "He is a noted lecturer and writer," she said, "an authority on nineteenth century Russian literature. I knew him rather well when we were young; it will be very nice to see him again— and his wife, of course." She hesitated, frowning thoughtfully. "I have heard that Mrs. Eltwing's mind is a little deranged; if she should seem—different, we must be very tactful."

We commenced right away to get the house in order for the Eltwing visit. "There will be a lot to do, Julia; I think we had better get Mrs. Peters to help us if she has the time." She stroked her chin in concentration. "I wonder if we should serve tea; Mrs. Eltwing is English, I believe. No, I think in spite of that, we'll serve coffee. Jonathan used to enjoy coffee and a special kind of cinnamon roll my mother made for him. Mamma was very fond of Jonathan until he outshone —someone very dear to her."

Uncle Haskell, I thought. Grandmother's fair-haired darling. I guessed that there was no love lost between Jonathan Eltwing and Uncle Haskell.

There was a pleasurable excitement in the air that week as we made our preparations. My grandmother's china had to be taken from the closet and each piece washed carefully and wiped. I was not allowed to breathe upon it, much less to touch it and so, with proper humility, I helped Mrs. Peters wax floors and wash windows, tasks in which my lack of coordination could do no particular damage. I didn't mind at all since I enjoyed working with Mrs. Peters; she was a chatty little woman, and a very good source of information regarding Aunt Cordelia and Jonathan Eltwing.

"Oh, they were in love, all right. She herself once admitted as much to me when we were young together," Mrs. Peters told me in a low voice as we washed the outside of the living room windows and kept on the lookout for any sudden appearance of Aunt Cordelia. "But after he left, the months went by, and she would have to say no to Jonathan's urging that she come to him—there was always sickness or debt or another worn-out old woman to be cared for. One couldn't blame Jonathan—he waited and hoped for a long time, and after a while I suppose that if the memory of her hurt, there were other women to soothe that hurt. I suppose I haven't any right to say this, Julie, but I'll say it anyway—if your grandfather had lived, things would have turned out differently around here. He would have seen to it that a certain person who shall be nameless would have carried his share of the burdens that fell upon this household. But not old Mrs. Bishop. Oh, no! According to her way of thinking, Cordelia was created to carry on for the rest of the family." Mrs. Peters paused for a few seconds and polished a pane of glass with a flash of energy out of all proportion to the need of her task. "I've said to Jim Peters many a time," she continued, "and he's always agreed with me, that old Mrs. Bishop was lacking in the qualities that make a good mother. And saying it that way makes her sound a good deal better than she really was."

By the week's end the whole house shone with the effects of ammonia and wax and furniture polish. On Saturday morning Aunt Cordelia allowed me to arrange several bowls of flowers for the piano and the mantel of the living room fireplace. "You show very good taste at that task, Julia," she said of my flower arrangements. There was an unmistakable air of graciousness about Aunt Cordelia that morning.

Fortunately it was chilly enough to warrant a fire in both fireplaces, and so we laid the kindling and wood, all ready to be lighted a half hour before our guests were expected. I polished the silver coffee service and set it on a low table in front of the fire, and Aunt Cordelia brought out a collection of little cakes and rolls which she had baked at ten that morning in order that they be oven-fresh.

The fires were crackling brightly at two-thirty, and the reflection of flame was deep in the polished mahogany lid of Uncle Haskell's grand piano, in the old wine decanter and the silver coffee service. Outside, the day was perfect with bright skies and the gay colors of our wooded surroundings. If Jonathan Eltwing had ever loved this old place, it must have wakened memories for him that afternoon.

Father drove up with Dr. and Mrs. Eltwing precisely at three o'clock; he knew Aunt Cordelia well enough to respect her passion for punctuality. I watched them walk up the brick-paved path to the porch where Aunt Cordelia stood waiting to greet them: Jonathan Eltwing so tall and huge as to dwarf my handsome and rather tall father; Mrs. Eltwing, a tiny, graceful woman wearing a pale gray velvet suit with a frilly blouse and a heavy gold pin at her throat. She had great, strangely brilliant eyes that dominated her tiny face and a mass of half-blonde, half-gray hair that she drew back smoothly from her forehead and wore in a great bun close to her neck. She was a lovely little creature with an air of childlike sweetness and innocence; she stood smiling and looking off into our bright woods as Jonathan Eltwing took Aunt Cordelia's hand in both his own and stood looking at her as if he were searching for the girl he had once known. I was proud of Aunt Cordelia; she looked slim and elegant standing there in the autumn sunlight, not once losing her cool composure as she greeted Jonathan Eltwing and his wife. I noticed that Father kissed her with special tenderness as if he understood that it was a difficult moment for her.

Then we were all in the living room in front of the fire. I sat close to Father, and watched the faces of those around me with keen interest.

Dr. Eltwing gave all of his attention at first to Aunt

Cordelia, asking her many questions, the two of them exchanging memories. Mrs. Eltwing seemed to pay no attention to any of us; she gave a little exclamation of pleasure over a plate of tidbits, and seating herself near it, picked up one piece after another, placing them quickly in her mouth and sucking off the grains of sugar or specks of frosting that clung to her fingers. There was somehow nothing greedy in her actions; each bit of food was held daintily, was bitten into with what seemed more like gay satisfaction than greed. Even the little gesture of removing the sugar from her fingers was done lightly and with a kind of merry charm. But the eating continued steadily until Dr. Eltwing held out his hands to her.

"Come and sit here beside me, Katy," he said gently. "I want to be sure that you understand who Miss Bishop is. Do you remember that I have often told you about the girl who tutored me when we were young, the one who helped me day after day until I was ready for my entrance examinations?"

Mrs. Eltwing uttered an amazed little "O-h-h" and turned to Aunt Cordelia in what seemed to be complete surprise. "Oh-h-h, I want to thank you—many, many times. You have been so good to my Jonathan." She hardly glanced at Aunt Cordelia as she spoke, but took the chair at her husband's side and looked up into his face as if to ask if she had said the right words.

Dr. Eltwing was very nice to me, once he got around to noticing that I was there. He was interested that I had read Tolstoi's *Anna Karenina,* and that I had tried to read Dostoievski's *Crime and Punishment,* but hadn't been able to get much out of it. He smiled a little at that admission.

"I think Dostoievski is pretty heavy fare for a young

lady of your age," he said. "Aren't you pushing her a little, Cordelia?"

"I haven't pushed her at all, Jonathan," Aunt Cordelia answered, "but I don't forbid her to browse either. She soon knows when she is beyond her depth."

"She pushed me, Julie; she really pushed me without mercy. And I've loved her for it—all these many years," he said quietly, and he was no longer smiling.

Aunt Cordelia's face was flushed, but she turned pleasantly to Mrs. Eltwing. "I know that you are a composer and a musician, Mrs. Eltwing. Do you feel like playing for us this afternoon? We've just had the piano tuned; I think you'll find it in good condition."

Mrs. Eltwing just smiled at Aunt Cordelia without answering until her husband bent down to her again. "Cordelia has asked if you will play for us, Katy. Do you feel up to it?"

She jumped eagerly to her feet as if he had interpreted a pleasant message in some foreign tongue. "Oh, yes, I'll play, Jonathan. Of course. Of course."

She walked lightly over to the piano bench, seated herself, and pushed back the cuffs of her velvet suit. It was then that I noticed the ruffle that extended from the sleeve of her blouse beyond the velvet cuff. It was torn and hung loosely; it was also a little soiled. A sad sign of her illness, I thought. No normal woman having the taste to groom herself so carefully in all other details would have overlooked that dangling ruffle.

In another minute, though, I had forgotten everything about me as Mrs. Eltwing poised her hands above the keys and then struck them as if in a wild fury. Waves of music crashed throughout the rooms of the old house, mountains began to shake and

comets to fall under her hands while I could imagine
tidal waves rolling in and the wind uprooting trees
and sending ships spinning to the bottom of the sea.
Then as my heart seemed almost ready to burst with
the tumult, her music suddenly subsided and the sky
became bright; the storm was over. The melody had
become quiet, but it was not happy; it seemed to
cry as if some lonely soul walked over the earth and
mourned the ravages that Nature had committed.

There was something eerie about Mrs. Eltwing as
she played. Her frail body swayed a little with the
music, her eyes that had looked so blue as she smiled
at us in greeting, were now quite black and brilliant
with light. She looked strange, and I felt for a moment
that I would be afraid to be alone with her.

Then it was over, and Mrs. Eltwing dropped her
hands into her lap. I was too moved to applaud,
but from the doorway between the library and living
room came a cry of "Bravo! Bravo!" and standing
there was Uncle Haskell, slender and graceful, clap-
ping his hands and smiling at Mrs. Eltwing.

I had never seen him look so handsome or so out-
landishly affected. He was wearing the black velvet
smoking jacket which he kept folded in layers of tissue
paper, and under that, a white silk shirt. His skin was
clear and firm, and his thick blond hair waved
back from a brow unmarked by either time or anxiety.
He looked a little like a foolish mannikin suddenly animated; he also looked a little like a Greek god. I
couldn't quite decide which description best fitted
him.

Mrs. Eltwing stood up at the sound of his cheering,
and she gave a little gasp as she looked at him. She
reminded me of a small girl who has suddenly discov-

ered an unbelievably beautiful toy; her eyes never left him as he came forward, took her hand lightly and kissed it.

"Thank you for that music, dear Mrs. Eltwing, thank you a million times. You have given me something precious just now, something infinitely precious."

Father looked strained as he always did when Uncle Haskell put in an appearance; Jonathan Eltwing's eyes had a preoccupied, brooding look; Aunt Cordelia did not move a muscle. Only Mrs. Eltwing looked pleased, even radiant. She did not say a word, but she looked at Uncle Haskell as if she had never seen a person so beautiful or so charming. When he turned to greet Dr. Eltwing, she continued to look at him, her eyes shining.

Uncle Haskell greeted Mr. Eltwing brusquely. "So good, Jonathan," he said, and our guest replied with a brusque greeting that matched the one he had received. Father and Uncle Haskell shook hands, nodded, and murmured something, nothing very cordial; then Aunt Cordelia invited her brother to sit down with us.

"Sorry, Cordelia, darling, I think I must get back to work. Deadline to meet by next week," he said, smiling at Mrs. Eltwing. "I'll have to be in New York for a conference with my publishers at the end of the week—events are crowding in on me a bit."

"Your book is coming out soon then?" Jonathan Eltwing asked politely.

"By spring, we hope," Uncle Haskell said airily. I was amazed at him. He knew that Father, Aunt Cordelia and I knew positively that he was lying, that Jonathan Eltwing was pretty well convinced of it, but these facts seemed not to affect him in the least. He had an audience of one person who believed him; sometimes I wondered if he didn't vaguely believe himself. He was not in the least embarrassed, but the rest of us were. I wondered how Aunt Cordelia had managed to stand it all through the years. I had had much less of Uncle Haskell than she had, and even I felt a little sick as I watched him.

"You will be staying in New York for some time, I suppose?" Jonathan Eltwing asked, mostly, I think, because it seemed necessary to say something when the silence became awkward.

"Only a week or ten days—at least I hope not any longer. I can't leave my girls alone too long, you know." He rumpled my hair, and I grinned inwardly. Aunt Cordelia and I could have been robbed, stabbed, drawn and quartered and Uncle Haskell would have known nothing about it. I wasn't too sure that he would have been greatly concerned, if he had known.

He went back to Mrs. Eltwing. "Thank you, thank you for a moment of pure delight, dear lady," he murmured. Then he bowed slightly to Dr. Eltwing. "So good, Jonathan," he said again. "Adam," he nodded at Father. "Until this evening, Cordelia—Julie, my sweetheart." Then he was gone, a flash of glory we were all relieved to see ended.

All but Mrs. Eltwing. She stood beside the piano looking after him, her face full of bewilderment and disappointment.

"Who was that man, Jonathan?" she asked her husband in a low voice, and we were all chagrined. Uncle Haskell's dramatic entrance had made us forget an introduction.

"That was Cordelia's brother, darling. Haskell Bishop."

"So beautiful," she said as if she were alone. "Such a beautiful and good man."

"Yes, Katy," Dr. Eltwing said gently. Then he turned to us, speaking quietly of other things.

The next hour was one of pleasant conversation in which everyone joined except Mrs. Eltwing. She sat close to her husband, leaning lightly against his shoulder, smiling a little to herself. I loved her somehow, and I really hadn't intended to, because she was the woman who had married the man my aunt had loved and I felt a certain loyalty to Aunt Cordelia. I loved Mrs. Eltwing, however, in spite of myself, mostly I think, because she was so tiny and delicate, so tragic. I believe that Dr. Eltwing saw the feeling in my eyes for he suddenly smiled at me, told me how fond he had been of my mother, hoped that I would visit him and his wife when they were settled in their new home. I was greatly flattered and pleased; it seemed to me something very special that I was a friend of Jonathan Eltwing.

But I spoiled it all as they were leaving. I smashed my hopes of a fine friendship as suddenly as I had smashed many a cup and plate in Aunt Cordelia's kitchen.

It happened as we stood on the wide porch saying good-bye. Dr. Eltwing held out his hand to me after he had shaken hands with Aunt Cordelia, and he said, "Good-bye, Julie, dear child. You know it's amazing how much you look like your Aunt Cordelia."

His words roused a quick fury inside me. I would have agreed with him that Aunt Cordelia looked rather nice that afternoon in her new golden colored wool with the brown velvet bow at her throat. But

she looked only nice for Aunt Cordelia, and I was
not flattered that I was compared to her, even when
she looked her best. I hadn't Laura's beauty, of
course, and that was a sore spot which had always
rankled, but I knew that I was prettier than Aunt
Cordelia. My cheeks were *not* thin and flat, my mouth
was *not* a thin, straight line, and my neck did *not* have
a strange, flabby fold running down the center. I hated
Dr. Eltwing at that minute. To humiliate me—me,
Julie Trelling in my new scarlet wool with a scarlet
velvet ribbon holding back my hair!

They were all looking at me, they were all seeing
the furious anger in my face. Father's face was red,
and his mouth looked hard; Aunt Cordelia was calm
with just the shadow of a smile on her lips; Mrs. Eltwing looked wistful, wondering. It was Jonathan
Eltwing's face that hurt me most. It had suddenly
become cold, severe. He dropped my hand and
nodded briefly. Then he turned to Aunt Cordelia and
did not look at me again.

I was completely miserable when Aunt Cordelia and
I came back into the living room. The cups with small
quantities of cold coffee in some of them did not
look so sparkling as they had that morning; the whole
room seemed cluttered; even the flowers I had arranged so proudly looked a little weary.

If Aunt Cordelia had given me the scolding of my
life I wouldn't have been either surprised or resentful.
I knew that I deserved one; I felt as if a few good
lashes would help me to live with myself. But she
didn't scold; she just sighed and shook her head as
she looked at the cups and plates.

"Somehow I don't quite feel up to washing them

right now." She smiled apologetically. Aunt Cordelia did not hold with people getting too tired to put a room to rights.

"I'll do them for you if you'll trust me," I said in a small voice. "I'll be terribly careful."

She looked at me absently for a moment and then nodded. "Yes, I know that you'll be careful. And if you *should* have an accident—maybe I have put too much value on a piece of china. Your wish to help me has value too." She went to the closet and took out an old sweater. "I think that I'll rake leaves for a while, Julia; the air smells so fresh. Maybe the exercise will do me good."

I changed my dress quickly and carried the dishes into the kitchen, lifting only one piece at a time into the soapy water, rinsing, wiping and setting it on the cupboard shelf before I picked up another. Then I swept up the crumbs and pushed the chairs back into their places, put more wood on the fire and carried the silver coffee service out to its place in the dining room. All during this time the tears were slipping over my cheeks; every so often I had to stop my work and use a handkerchief.

It was an empty, shamed and remorseful evening, terrible really. I stood at the window for a long time when my work was done and watched Aunt Cordelia as she raked up great piles of leaves and pushed them into a deep ditch that ran on one side of our woodsy lawn. It was so foolish to be raking leaves at that time, a completely futile gesture, for the trees were still full of leaves, and as quickly as Aunt Cordelia raked one section of the lawn, it was again covered with the bright rain from the boughs above. It was a foolish expenditure of energy—that is what Aunt Cordelia would ordinarily have said to me had I been occupied by this pointless task.

Another thing struck me: Aunt Cordelia had not changed her best dress before going out to work among the dusty leaves. It was unprecedented behavior on her part. Not on mine. I often forgot, and I had been reprimanded many a time for my negligence. And now, there was Aunt Cordelia hard at work in her best dress, her fragile stockings and high heels. I wouldn't have believed it possible.

Darkness came to our house sooner than it did elsewhere because of the many trees surrounding us. I watched the sunset, hardly brighter than the leaves had been that afternoon, and I thought that surely Aunt Cordelia would soon come inside. I started a kettle of water heating slowly for tea and I planned to make hot buttered toast and scrambled eggs when I saw her putting her rake in the tool shed. But I waited and waited, and when she set fire to the great piles of leaves she had raked together and the blue-gray coils of smoke started rolling, I knew that she would stay outside until every leaf in the ditch was burned and every ember carefully extinguished.

It was quite dark when Aunt Cordelia came inside, her hair disarranged and her face and dress grimed lightly with the smoke. If I had been in a different mood, I might have gloated over the fact that it was her carelessness, not mine, that was going to cost us a cleaning bill the next week. But I was not in a mood for gloating; my spirit was too much abased.

"You have made tea, Julia? Good. I'll be down as soon as I've changed and freshened up a little." She glanced at her smudged skirt and then looked at me with a wry little smile. "I've been very foolish, Julia.

Somehow I forgot to change. I must remember this before I scold you when you forget."

I wanted to say, "Don't be kind to me. Hit me; scream at me. It will make me feel better." But, of course, she did no such thing. She went upstairs, quick and light of step, and I prepared our little snack which I carried into the living room and set in front of the fire. I then turned on two shaded lamps and sat down to wait for her.

She came down soon, wearing the long rose-colored robe that was her favorite, and carrying a large manila envelope which meant, I supposed, that she was going to spend the evening working on her household bills. When she had seated herself in an armchair before the fire, she drew a long breath and reached for a piece of toast.

"This is very nice," she said quietly, "I didn't realize that I was hungry, but I am."

I tried to begin the little apology I had been working on all evening. I cleared my throat and began shakily, "Aunt Cordelia, I want to say—"

Then she did an amazing thing: she interrupted me. Interrupting another's speech was almost as horrendous an act in Aunt Cordelia's code as neglecting one's homework or calling Jane Austen a bore.

"Mrs. Eltwing is a pathetic little woman, isn't she, Julia? So lovely, so gifted—and so lost. Did you notice how exceptionally kind and understanding Jonathan is? But he was always like that—the gentlest and best person I have ever known."

I felt that for some reason she did not want me to voice an apology, and so I sat beside her, feeling very wretched and awkward, trying to eat a little of the food for which I had no appetite.

Aunt Cordelia took her time over the meal, sipping her tea slowly and helping herself to a second piece of toast. When she had finally finished she wiped her fingers carefully on her napkin, and getting up, she reached for the envelope on the mantel.

"I've had this in my bureau drawer, Julia. I should have shown it to you before. It would have helped you to understand this afternoon."

She drew out a sepia colored photograph, rather faded but still clear, of a young man and woman and a younger child. I knew in a flash who it was. The blond, graceful young man standing in the rear with his face turned carefully, no doubt in order to give posterity the full benefit of his beautiful profile, could be no one other than Uncle Haskell. And the child, leaning against the young woman's knee and smiling directly into the camera looked like a miniature Laura, but was, of course, my mother.

However, it was the young woman seated on the photographer's velvet-covered bench that held my attention. The other two I would have recognized, but not the lovely girl in the center. Her head was thrown back a little as if some word that had brought the smile to her pretty lips had also brought the small oval chin up in a mood of gayety. Her cheeks were full and rounded, her dark hair was brushed back but little curls had sneaked out at her temples. And the neck—that girlish neck was smooth and firm; there was a thin black ribbon tied around it and a small heart rested in the hollow of her throat.

"This was taken the first year I taught," Aunt Cordelia said in a matter-of-fact voice. "That was the year that Jonathan and I worked together to prepare him for his entrance examinations."

Of course. That was the year. And no doubt the photographer had said coyly, "Now think of someone you love, and let's have a big smile." And she had thought of Jonathan Eltwing; you could almost see his image in her large, dark eyes.

I put the photograph on the arm of my chair and then I knelt and buried my head in her lap. I seldom touched Aunt Cordelia; she never invited demonstrative behavior, but that night as I shook with sobs, she patted my shoulder and smoothed my hair back from my forehead.

"I'm a beast, Aunt Cordelia, an ungrateful, bad-mannered beast. I'm cruel and hateful—"

She gave my shoulder a little shake. "Now, now, that's enough. Let's have no more of this." She lifted my face with her hand under my chin and looked at me with a little smile. "You're neither cruel nor mean; basically, you are a very good child. You're just young," she added, and it was as if she said the last words to herself.

Chapter Six

My last year in elementary school was Aunt Cordelia's last year of teaching. The decision to leave her position was not her own; rural schools were being consolidated that year, and children who would have learned under Aunt Cordelia were taken by bus into the town schools. The white schoolhouse where she had taught for forty years was sold at auction and used for the storage of grain.

Aunt Cordelia was very quiet as talk of these changes went through the community. She didn't approve of many things she heard of the teachers in the town schools. They were a permissive lot, and Aunt Cordelia believed that children were happier if the boundaries of their behavior were established early and they knew exactly where they stood with reference to authority; neither did she approve of something called "social studies," which she felt was a hodgepodge of watered down ideas being substituted for honest and scholarly courses in history and geography.

When she was invited to take a class in town, she refused promptly. "I have taught in my own way, following the dictates of my own judgment for too many years," she said. "The philosophy and the restrictions of city schools would be too much for me." So saying she gave up her profession, and no one was ever quite sure just how she felt about it.

She brought home the brass handbell from her desk, the framed pictures of many groups of children with which she had decorated the drab walls of the classroom, and a great stack of old class rosters dating back to the year when Eltwing, Jonathan, was one of the names inscribed. I spent hours going through those lists of names with her.

"Trevort, Charles," I read. Danny's father. A fine boy, Aunt Cordelia said. One of the younger ones. It had only been a very few years in her reckoning since Trevort, Charles, had helped her with the heavy coal buckets and the Monday morning fires as Danny had done in my time.

Aunt Cordelia read the names with me and commented upon the personalities. "That girl had a way with words when she was no more than six; she's published three volumes of poetry so far. I'm not surprised; I recognized her gift." Or, "Now that one was bound for trouble from the first. She was boy crazy before she was quite aware that there *were* two sexes."

She remembered them all; she had indicated the universities to which some of them had gone, the careers many of them had followed, the persons they had married. The word "deceased" was written after many names. "Kilpin, Agnes—deceased," I read on a late roster.

As autumn approached that year everyone supposed

that Aunt Cordelia would be very sad. It was the first September since she was six years old that she had not entered a classroom either as a student or a teacher. "She will be lost," the family feared. "She will be heartsick and lonely."

But Aunt Cordelia didn't seem heartsick. "When the first day of school comes this September," she told me, "I intend to stand quietly in the sunlight and lay my hands on the bark of one of the tallest trees. I'll say to myself, 'Well, good! Now *that* part of my life is finished.' And after that I may gather an armful of autumn flowers, and I'll move slowly while I do it and breathe deeply of good, clean air that is free of chalk dust. Maybe I'll make peach preserves in the afternoon or reread a few chapters of *Pride and Prejudice;* I may take a long walk in the woods or call on Helen Trevort or Cora Peters. I may fix a nice dinner for Jonathan and Katy Eltwing. Whatever I do, it will be as I please, and I intend to savor every minute of it."

Aunt Cordelia didn't talk like that ordinarily. She seemed to be anticipating her freedom in September, and yet I couldn't quite believe it. It struck me uncomfortably that if it *were* true, she might be also anticipating the fact that she was getting rid of me as well as the labor and problems and smells of a country classroom. She hadn't once mentioned my leaving her —no little moan for Julie.

I had overheard remarks that summer. "Being responsible for an adolescent is too much; Cordelia has done her share." And again, "Julie is a dear child, but —well, you know—temperamental, a bit headstrong, impetuous. And there will be the boy-problem before long and all the turmoil of growing up. It's too much to ask of Cordelia now that she is getting old."

And so, in spite of all the plans I had for the years

in high school, I felt a wave of wistfulness. Aunt Cordelia was waiting to be free of me, perhaps was good and tired of me. It hurt. I couldn't help it; it bothered me.

Of course I was eager to go home. In my desk drawers were little calendars that I had made from time to time, with notations of the number of years, months and days until I would be old enough to be free of Aunt Cordelia's lectures, her stern routine of duties, her authoritarian attitude. I had long looked forward to the day when I would no longer be a "country girl," when I would be living with a parent rather than an elderly aunt not too much admired by many of my peers, when I would have Laura's old room where I could look out over the flower garden that seemed to evoke Mother's presence.

I had visited Father frequently during my years with Aunt Cordelia, and the visits were nearly always a delight, a foretaste of the life we'd lead when I was in high school and also Father's "hostess" as Laura had been. We often went out to eat, because Father liked to take advantage of any excuse to get away from the food served by his housekeeper, Mrs. Coffers, who was certainly a wretched cook, but so old, and so unskilled that she couldn't find another job. She thus escaped being dismissed, because Father was unable to hurt anyone unfortunate and helpless.

"I really must take my little girl out for a celebration, Mrs. Coffers," he would say, and the old woman would give us a gimlet-eyed look that made me suspect she knew the real reason behind our visit to an expensive restaurant. She didn't believe in squandering money on "high living," she grunted, and wondered since when professors in small state colleges earned salaries that allowed them to go out and buy lobster when fried steak and canned peas in white sauce made a meal good enough for anyone.

But Father and I dined out often all the same, and I felt very proud to follow the head waiter along a thickly carpeted dining room with my well-dressed and distinguished-looking father close behind me. When we were seated, I studied the menu with what I hoped was a slightly bored air, although I nearly always grew excited over the strange, delicious dishes and it was difficult to hide my enthusiasm. Then as Father gave our orders, I daintily drew off my gloves, one finger at a time and wondered if people around us thought that I was sixteen—possibly older—and was dining with some elderly admirer. Father was always amused, and I greatly enjoyed my acting until one night a sudden realization of what I was doing struck me.

"Father, am I like Uncle Haskell?" I asked him in consternation.

He patted my hand reassuringly. "Acting is rather good fun, Julie, if it isn't carried too far; Uncle Haskell went overboard with his acting a very long time ago, but I don't think you need to worry. Your reasons for it are quite different from his." Then he frowned at me slightly. "Still, I'm glad that you've recognized a pattern; think about it if you ever feel yourself getting carried away."

Often he read to me when we sat before the fire in his study, and we discussed the books that I had read, and I tingled with delight at his pleasure in my understanding. Once he took me to a faculty reception where he danced with me and some of his male graduate students made quite a fuss over me. Aunt Cordelia had a bit of a time getting my head out of the clouds after that experience.

I always slept in Laura's old room. It was the prettiest room upstairs, where I had often gone late at night when I was little, pretending that I'd had a bad dream so that Laura would take me into her bed and kiss me and comfort me. Now, when I visited Father I would sleep in Laura's room and I would pretend that my hair, scattered across the pillow, was thick, rippling gold like my sister's. I'd pretend that Mother was still alive and that I, being much the oldest daughter, was Mother's confidante; that I had a younger brother and sister, whom I loved very much.

Quite often on these visits Alicia Allison was invited to be with us. She was as pretty as when I first knew her, and always beautifully dressed; there was a gayety about Alicia that made her seem almost as young as Laura. It was obvious that Father liked her; and I noticed that she now called him "Adam"; when she had talked to him at Laura's wedding, she had called him "Dr. Trelling."

I was long past the pettishness I had shown when Laura suggested that it was about time Father married Alicia and got me away from Uncle Haskell's influence. I liked her; furthermore, I thought that it might be advantageous for me to claim the highly popular Miss Allison for my stepmother when I entered high school. I certainly was not jealous of her; actually I rather looked forward to the day when the three of us would live together.

We went ice-skating during the winter, Alicia, Father and I, or we took long tramps through the snowy woods and then came back to her small cottage where we drank spiced cider and munched the pleasant little pastries she had prepared for us. On a few occasions I spent the night with her, and we talked of frivolous things like face creams and the weight one should be for her height, and once she let me do her hair a new way and seemed really pleased with the effect. They were the kind of evenings one would never spend with Aunt Cordelia.

Then, finally, the spring before I was to enter high school, Alicia and Father were married. It was a quiet wedding, but a very lovely one. Laura and Bill were there with little Julie; Danny escorted Aunt Cordelia, and besides these, Dr. and Mrs. Eltwing, Mr. and Mrs. Trevort and a few faculty couples made up the guest list. Chris was Father's best man, and I was Alicia's one attendant. It was very nice of Alicia to ask me; the honor might well have gone to Laura, because Alicia and my sister had been close friends since Laura's high school days. But she chose me, and Laura seemed pleased; I had the feeling that the two of them had talked it over. Anyway I was happy in my important role, and much impressed with the ankle-length dress which Alicia had bought for me.

We had fun that summer. I was to move in with them at the beginning of school when the redecorating of our old house was completed; until then I often visited them for the weekend, and it was a delight. Mostly. It wasn't quite as much fun to go to a restaurant with Alicia and Father as it had been to go with him alone. There was no longer any doubt but that I was just some outsized kid tagging along and that she was Father's dinner companion. She and Father could have wine together and touch their glasses over some private little toast; they offered to buy me a carbonated drink so that I could join them, but I re-

fused. It seemed rather artificial; too much like Uncle
Haskell's *Le Vieux Corbeau.*

Most of the time, however, everything was perfect.
Like one night when we had come home late from a
movie, and Father had declared that he was starved
and Alicia and I were suddenly ravenous too. We had
cooked hamburgers and coffee, and Alicia had whirled
up a milkshake for me. Then we had talked until we
were half dead with sleepiness and Alicia had said,
"Oh, bother with the dishes," and we had put them in
the sink to wait until morning. That might not have
been a thing of any importance to many girls, but it
impressed me, because never, in all the years that I
had been with Aunt Cordelia, had we fixed a snack
late at night; most certainly, we had never left a dish
unwashed in the sink. "What if illness should strike
in the night?" Aunt Cordelia had said to me once
when I wanted to leave the very few dishes we had
used at supper until the next morning. "What if
strangers came into our home and saw evidences of
such slothful habits?"

I told Aunt Cordelia of the fun we had had with
our midnight meal and our unconcern with evidence
of slothful habits.

"You mean, Julia, that you enjoy coming down to a
disheveled kitchen when you get up of a morning?"
she asked.

"It isn't *that,* Aunt Cordelia, it isn't the cooking at
midnight or leaving the dishes. It's just—" I tried to
find the right words. "It's just the flexibility of a way
of living."

Aunt Cordelia raised her brows. I had used the
words "inflexible" a time or two when we had had an

altercation. She understood me perfectly—but we still washed the dishes every night!

But little things happened at the house in town that summer, things of no special importance, but the sum of them began to bother me. One thing was the mirror. It really was of little moment, but it made me realize that there were adjustments which I would have to make now that there was a new mistress in our home.

The mirror had hung in the living room for as long as I could remember, a beautifully cut glass just above the back of the davenport; Chris and I used to stand there when we were little and play with our reflections in the faintly blue depths that made us look a little strange, a little like children in some softly illustrated fairy tale. Alicia decided to move the mirror; she thought it would look better over the buffet in the dining room.

"But Mother always—" I began in a rather severe tone, and then stopped myself.

Alicia smiled at me. "I know, Julie, I know very well how you feel. But your mother and I were very good friends. She would want me to arrange the house to my taste, I feel quite sure."

Well, I wondered! But it was a little thing. Later I told Alicia that the mirror did, indeed, look nice in the dining room and she seemed pleased.

After we had removed the mirror, it was plain that the walls needed redecorating, and when they were done in a beautiful French gray, Alicia confided in me that she was going to be profligate and buy the outrageously expensive draperies that she had long wanted. We had a wonderful time selecting them together, and it was pleasant to find that our tastes were quite similar. We bought a heavy tapestry the color of the walls but brightened by great irregular splashes of cerise, a bold color that delighted both of us.

We were all quite pleased with the effect in the living room, but when the kitchen was done over, and the old dining table under which Chris and I used to hide and pinch Father's ankles while he dined, was discarded in favor of one very smart and modern, I felt as if this were no longer my home. I got a lonely feeling in it, although I had to admit that it was beautiful.

But it was Laura's room that mattered most. Somehow, it had never entered my mind that this room would be other than mine. It had belonged to me in every dream that I'd had of coming home; later I thought how strange it is that your dreams can be so real as to make you sure that other people are aware of them too.

I seemed to feel faint warnings of a deeper shock to come when, on one weekend visit, I found that Alicia had had Mother's old flower garden put to sod so that it stretched out as a continuation of the green lawn.

"Don't you think it makes the lawn lovelier, Julie?" Alicia asked, apparently certain that I would agree with her. "The garden hasn't really been carefully tended for so long and was actually getting very shabby. If either your father or I had green thumbs— but we don't. Neither green thumbs, nor time for gardening, if we're to get term papers and final examinations graded."

"Yes, I think it's an improvement—I do, really,

Alicia." I tried to make my voice enthusiastic, but my dream was beginning to be upset. The view of the flower garden from Laura's window was part of the memory I wanted back.

Later, Alicia wanted to show me what she had been doing to the rooms upstairs. That's when I saw Laura's room.

The white curtains were gone, and draperies of coarsely woven cloth in blue and copper were at the windows. The shell-pink walls had become beige and gold, and a thick beige carpet covered the floor which Laura had always left bare with fluffy white throw-rugs here and there. The pink and white bed was gone too, and the only furnishings in the room were a massive walnut desk with a special niche for a typewriter, a few straight chairs and several bookshelves against the walls.

"My home office," Alicia said with a pleased sigh. "Your father has the library—I insisted that he keep it to himself; up here I'll wield my red pencil over high-school themes and when I finally explode, at least I'll do it in privacy. I'd hate for you or your father to see me when I begin pulling my hair—"

I couldn't keep from wailing, "Oh, Alicia, *what* have you done?"

She was amazed. "But Julie, your father told me that this was Laura's room—not yours. I'm having your own little room all done over with a matching desk and bookcase and draperies that I think are the loveliest. I thought I'd be making you so happy—I didn't dream—"

Well, there were reassurances and apologies and more reassurances until finally I convinced Alicia that I was, of course, delighted with my old room and

that she should never think of my outburst again.
Everything was settled, but that night we were a little
quieter than usual at our meal, and Alicia and Father
glanced at one another as if they were thinking that it
certainly was too much of a chore for Aunt Cordelia
to look after a girl of my age; that they saw it as being
something of a problem even for themselves.

During the next few weeks everything went
smoothly; then one morning I came downstairs in my
house slippers and walked into the breakfast nook
without their hearing me. It really wasn't anything—
just a recently married husband and wife giving one
another an exceptionally warm embrace and good-
morning kiss. Nothing wrong with that, but it was
their surprise, their sudden standing apart with a half-
embarrassed, half-irritated look that struck me full
force. I said, "Oh, excuse me," and they said, "Not at
all, dear," and we all laughed a little, and they poked
a bit of fun at themselves for romancing before breakfast.

But the experience left a strange feeling inside me;
it wasn't the jealousy I had felt at Laura's, for I
certainly wasn't trying to stand in the Number One
place with either Alicia or Father. It was, rather, the
feeling that I didn't belong anywhere—not in a house
that was no longer my old home but a beautiful,
strange place where I might at any moment invade
the privacy of two people very much in love; not at
Aunt Cordelia's if it was true that I had become a
burden to her.

I went out from town on the rickety old bus that
passed within a mile of home that afternoon. It
seemed strange that I should think of Aunt Cordelia's
place as "home"; always before it was the house in

town that had been closest in my affection. But as I walked the dusty mile from bus-stop to the old house in the woods I thought about my room at Aunt Cordelia's with more warmth than I ever had before. It was twice as large as my old one in town, and while the furnishings were old, they were mellow and held more significance for me than did the desk and bookcase that Alicia had selected for me. Aunt Cordelia and I had worked together refinishing my bureau, a walnut one that had been old even when she was a child; I knew how much sanding and rubbing and polishing had been necessary to bring out the beauty of the fine wood. It suddenly seemed to me that I couldn't bear to give up my beautiful old furniture for the glossy new things that should have been giving me so much happiness.

I wondered, too, how it would seem waking up of a morning and being unable to look out at the woods, my beloved woods that were hardly the same two days in succession. There would be a veil of fog one morning, and bright sunlight or gray rain the next; there would be snowy branches, or little, tender, new leaves, or colorful autumn ones—always a new picture to put away in my memory. I wanted my woods as I wanted my big room and my old bureau. I wanted, too, the freedom of the old house where I could run through the many rambling, high-ceilinged rooms singing if I cared to sing, exploring some ancient trunk or nook or closet that I had missed, never wondering if I were going to startle two persons burdened with someone like me in too small a house. For the first time, I was conscious of Aunt Cordelia's home as a haven, and I wanted desperately to know that I was welcome there.

Uncle Haskell called to me as I walked up the long

driveway. "Well, Julie, my sweet, are you happy at the prospect of shaking the dust of this estate from your little feet?"

I linked my arm in his, and we walked on up the path without my answering. Uncle Haskell seldom noticed whether one replied to his remarks or not; he was interested only in his own voice.

"And how are the impeccable Adam and his beautiful bride?" he asked maliciously.

"Quite well. Not wholly impeccable, but they're both very nice people," I answered.

He bent down suddenly and looked into my face. "Come to think of it, you look a bit drawn, my pet. What is it? Were you pushed a little backstage away from the footlights?"

I thought, "That is *your* idea of pain, isn't it, dear Uncle?" But I said, "There's not a thing wrong except for that old bus and the ghastly heat." And then I changed the subject. "How is the magnum opus coming along?"

"Beautifully," he answered, smiling blandly and without the slightest embarrassment or anger. "Magnificently, really. I'm very pleased—so much so that I think I'll go out for a spot of twilight golf this evening. One must relax a bit, you know."

"Of course," I agreed, going along with the time-honored hokum. "Have a good game." We smiled at one another and parted at the end of the lane. Uncle Haskell and I had a tepid sort of liking for one another.

The drawn look that he had noticed in my face must very well have been evident, for as Aunt Cordelia and I sat in the living room that evening, she looked at me in her direct way and plunged into my anxiety bluntly.

"Tell me all about it, Julia," she said without prelude.

I had not told her about the little things that had bothered me, the mirror and especially Laura's room. They seemed to show up a childishness in me that I didn't like. But the breakfast-nook incident was different; it pointed up their discomfiture as well as mine. I tried to show in my telling of it that I held no rancor, only a sense of insecurity, of loneliness.

Aunt Cordelia nodded when I was through. "I think I understand how you feel, though I believe that you have misinterpreted Adam and Alicia. It's unfortunate that in our culture, where the accent is so much upon youth, that people of middle age feel awkward and absurd if they demonstrate their love. They feel that they're playing a role that belongs to nobody over thirty. I'd guess that is how your parents felt this morning—a kind of embarrassment rather than annoyance."

I thought for a while. "I'm egotistical, isn't that it, Aunt Cordelia? And egotistical people are supersensitive, aren't they?"

Aunt Cordelia smiled. "In a few years you'll love someone, Julia, and it will make a great difference in you. You'll see. A woman is never completely developed until she has loved a man; when that happens in the right way she is happy in other people's love as well as her own; she is more generous and understanding about the feelings of others. You might say that she knows completeness."

Then I asked a question that I shouldn't have, one

that might well have brought me a rebuff, although it
didn't.

"Did you feel that completeness the year—the first
year you taught, Aunt Cordelia?"

I was immediately full of consternation at having
asked the question, but to my surprise, she answered
me readily.

"Yes," she said, "I did."

We were silent for a while, during which time my
worry over a home came uppermost in my thoughts.

"Am I a pain in the neck, Aunt Cordelia?" I asked
finally.

She came quickly from the "woman who had known
completeness" to the spinsterish schoolteacher.

"I dislike that expression very much, Julia; it is
flippant and in poor taste. However, I fully understand
your meaning, of course. No, you are neither trouble-
some nor an annoyance to me."

"I thought that maybe I was getting to an age
where I am too great a responsibility," I quoted.

"I never said that. Laura and Adam and Alicia decided that."

"You wouldn't mind if I stayed here then—if I lived
with you while I'm in high school. I'll try to be ma-
ture, Aunt Cordelia, honestly I'll try. I don't want to be
a burden, but when you get down to brass tacks, this
is *home* so far as I'm concerned."

Aunt Cordelia closed her eyes for a second and
shook her head ever so slightly. But she was smiling
as she made the gesture; I had never seen her look
like that before.

"If you choose to stay with me, Julia, I shall be
much, much happier this fall than I had expected to
be. You have come to seem like my own child, and I

haven't wanted to think of what it would be like this winter with no girl coming in from school, no young mind to guide—" She stopped then, apparently troubled. "How are Adam and Alicia going to feel about this, Julia? They've been expecting you, getting things ready for you. Are they going to feel hurt?"

My spirit was soaring. I would be a part of the old, the familiar. The roots that I had put down during the past six years need not be disturbed. I could be realistic about Father and Alicia without pain: they would welcome me, of course, if I moved into town, but they wouldn't suffer any sharp agony if I only came in for an occasional weekend. And that was all right. Don't try to get into the Number One place, my girl. Father and Alicia had as much right to their privacy as had Laura and Bill. Anyway, I had Aunt Cordelia.

"I'll make them understand." I tried to put into words the feeling I had for Father and Alicia: "I like them very much, Aunt Cordelia; I admire them too, but it's as if they are sort of holiday parents. Everything is just fine and new and beautiful; we're all polite and careful of one another's feelings. But they'll just have to understand: you and I are closer."

Aunt Cordelia sat very straight in her chair for a long time without speaking. Then she said quite casually, "Well, I suppose we'd better get to our beds. Be sure to hang your dress up properly, Julia; you left some of your things lying about the room when you left for the weekend."

It was cool and quiet and wonderful in my room. I lay in the wide old bed between my two windows, and looked up at the stars which were thick above the trees that night. This was home, this was contentment, a warm and good contentment in spite of the fact that

I knew in winter the room would be icy and I'd have to leap downstairs to dress beside one of the big stoves, in spite of the fact that I would not be one of the townclique and so would probably have fewer beaux, in spite of the fact that I knew there would be altercation between Aunt Cordelia and me. It didn't matter. Here on the wall were the bookshelves that my grandfather had made for Aunt Cordelia when she was young; out in the stable there was Peter the Great, getting old, but still showing his blood; there were the country roads and the woods; there was good old Danny down the road, and silly little Carlotta.

I thought about things Aunt Cordelia and I had talked about that evening. Especially love. I wondered if I would ever love anyone; if any boy would ever love me. I wondered what it would be like to have a boy's kiss—oh, not that silly kid-play of Danny's when Chris and Jimmie held my arms. What interested me were the kisses I read about or the ones I had watched with a kind of a hypnotized distaste when I had seen them in the movies. I wondered what it was like to be married, and then I wondered about babies and the bits I'd heard here and there. Once I had asked Laura shortly after little Julie was born, "Was it very dreadful, Laura?" And she had answered, just as bright and sparkling as she usually was those days, "Not really, darling. A bit rough for a few hours and after that, pure joy." I wanted a baby very much, one that was all mine, beautiful and soft. I wanted to be grown up and to know all about the things I wondered about. I sighed and turned in my bed luxuriously. "I do so want to be complete," I thought.

Chapter Seven

Dr. Jonathan Eltwing did not forgive easily. I soon learned that he would not be quick in forgetting my behavior on that day when he and his wife first called on us, and I knew that I couldn't blame him. I admired and respected the huge, sad-eyed scholar who was equally kind to Aunt Cordelia and to his sad little wife, but it was a long time before he was anything but cool and distant toward me.

The Eltwings had established themselves in a pleasant old house about three miles from Aunt Cordelia's, shortly after their initial visit to us. It was as lonely and isolated as ours, but much smaller and out of keeping with the handsome furnishings they had sent out from the East. People wondered what had brought Jonathan Eltwing back to our part of the country after so many years in which he had apparently forgotten his birthplace. No one was ever quite sure although it was generally believed that he had sought out a place where he could shield his wife

from curious eyes and tongues. Mrs. Peters had her
own idea which she confided to me. "Sometimes old
memories have a strong pull, Julie. I can't say this
to many people, but it's my own conviction that
Jonathan Eltwing has never been able to forget the
winter he and Cordelia were eighteen."

Whatever the reason for their return, they were a
sad and tragic couple. Within a few months after
their arrival, it was obvious that the state of Katy
Eltwing's mind was worsening. She was fearful when
neighbors called in the casual, friendly way of country people; sometimes she strayed from home and
had been found, frightened and bewildered, in the
adjacent fields and woods. The housekeeper from
town gossiped of days when Mrs. Eltwing sat at the
piano and wept because her hands had lost their
skill; she told how Jonathan Eltwing would leave his
work to hold the distraught woman in his arms,
soothing and comforting her until she forgot her sorrow.

Often when his wife was safely under the care of
others, Jonathan would come down to Aunt Cordelia's
and sit before the fire, talking quietly with her, sometimes leaning his head against the back of the chair
as if he savored a tranquil moment removed from
care. He spoke politely to me on these occasions, but
that was all; he never saw Uncle Haskell nor did he
ever ask of him. My uncle and I did not share Aunt
Cordelia's place in the affection of our new neighbor.

There came an autumn night of fog and mist just a
year after the Eltwings' arrival, however, when it was
necessary for Jonathan Eltwing to talk to Uncle Haskell and to me.

It was on one of those rare occasions when Aunt

Cordelia had gone into town to attend a lecture with Father and Alicia. I was up in my room polishing off the last of my homework when I heard Uncle Haskell's voice, its habitual jauntiness submerged in anxiety.

"Julie, come down quickly," he called, and I ran downstairs wondering at the note of alarm in his tone. Once outside in the dooryard I understood his concern, for there, holding his hand as if she were a child clinging to a parent, was Mrs. Eltwing. Her grayish blonde hair, dampened by the mist, had come unpinned and fell in a tangle about her face and shoulders. Those shoulders were bare, still beautiful in spite of mud and scratches, and they rose from what had once been a lovely dress of blue velvet, now torn in a dozen places by brambles or underbrush that she had encountered, the long full skirt splashed halfway to her waist by mud and water.

"She was in the middle of the old creek bridge," Uncle Haskell told me in a low voice. "She was crying—afraid to come on across or to turn back. See if you can take care of her, Julie." He was as agitated as if someone had placed a day-old infant in his arms.

I knew the creek bridge. It was narrow and without railings. When the creek was high, as it was that night, the dilapidated old crossing seemed a little hazardous even to sure-footed kids such as Danny and I were. I felt a rush of sympathy for the lost woman who had attempted to make that crossing alone and in the night, but when I tried to take her hand in order to lead her inside, she cried out shrilly, refusing to allow me to touch her, and turning to Uncle Haskell as if for protection.

He led her inside while I ran to the telephone and

called her husband. "I'll be there," Jonathan Eltwing said as soon as I spoke his wife's name; I heard him drop the receiver without bothering to put it back on its hook.

In the living room I turned on the lights and Uncle Haskell helped the disheveled woman into an armchair where he stood looking down at her, apparently perplexed and uncertain as to what he should do next. Mrs. Eltwing looked up at him, and the fright seemed to leave her eyes as if she suddenly recognized a friend. The light shone on tiny beads of mist that covered Uncle Haskell's blond hair; she seemed to be fascinated by them.

"Beautiful—beautiful," she whispered after a while. "You are a kind and beautiful man. I am not afraid now." She took his hand and pressed it against her cheek.

Uncle Haskell glanced at me in consternation. "Dear Mrs. Eltwing," he stammered, "dear little lady—"

She apparently did not notice his discomfiture, but continued to look at him as if just seeing him gave her complete happiness. If it had not been for the sadness of her condition, I could have laughed at his incredulous and frantic expression.

I noticed that her slippers were gone, that her feet in the torn stockings she wore were cut and bleeding. I brought a basin of warm water and a soft towel, but when I prepared to bathe her feet she again resisted me and turned imploringly to Uncle Haskell.

He hesitated when I extended the basin toward him; I doubt if Grandmother Bishop's darling had ever performed a personal service for anyone, but after a few seconds, he knelt before Katy Eltwing and bathed and dried her little feet as tenderly as Father would have done for me under like circumstances.

He was still kneeling on the floor, touching the cuts on her feet with iodine which I had brought from the medicine chest when Jonathan Eltwing ran up the porch steps and into the living room. His face looked haggard as he bent over his wife and lifted her in his arms.

"Katy—Katy, I thought you were sleeping," he said brokenly. "Poor little girl, I never dreamed—"

"The golden haired man found me, Jonathan—I wasn't afraid after he found me. But I'm so tired—so tired. I think you'd better take me home, darling."

He laid her on a couch in the library and sat beside her, soothing and reassuring her for a long time. Finally he came back into the living room, closing the door softly behind him.

"She is asleep," he said with heavy sigh. He slumped down in an armchair without looking at either Uncle Haskell or me. "Where is Cordelia?" he asked abruptly.

"She's in town with Father and Alicia," I answered. "They'll probably be bringing her home in a little while."

He nodded. "Now tell me, Haskell, where did you find Katy? What happened?"

His voice was harsh with dislike. I glanced at Uncle Haskell quickly, half expecting a stinging reply, but he answered Dr. Eltwing civilly although with an unmistakable coldness.

"I had gone for a walk down toward the creek. I heard crying from the bridge. I went to her, brought her here as you can see."

"Did she recognize you?"

"No, it was quite dark in the woods. We have only met the one time; she could have had no idea who I was. I'm sure of that."

"But she allowed you to take her hand—to lead her?"

"Yes. She was like a lost child, happy to be rescued."

Dr. Eltwing ran his hand across his forehead. "I can't understand. For months she has allowed no one to touch her except me, even when she has been lost and frightened. And yet, she allowed you to lead her —to wash the cuts on her feet."

I felt a little sick. I thought that if this sorry business fed Uncle Haskell's ego, that if he boasted of the special place he held in this deranged woman's feelings, I would die of shame for him. I watched his face to see if I could read his reactions.

But there was nothing in his face that night to substantiate my fears. He stood there, silent and perplexed, as he looked down at Jonathan Eltwing's bent head. For the first time, I thought that he looked old.

Finally he said, "If it will help her—if my listening to her music will make her happy—" he broke off and started for the door. "Feel free to call on me if I can help her, Jonathan," he called back, and was gone.

Dr. Eltwing did not talk to me after Uncle Haskell left. He went into the library and, lifting his wife in his arms, carried her as if she were a sleeping child, down the long lane to his car. I followed with a soft pillow from the couch, and when he had placed his wife in a half-reclining position on the seat, I adjusted the pillow beneath her head and shoulders. Then I looked up at his sad face as he stood watching me, and for a second I forgot that he was "Dr."

Eltwing and that, in any case, I was too young to address him by his given name. But before I realized it, the name had slipped out.

"She will be all right now, Jonathan," I said.

Dr. Eltwing apparently forgot something too. He said, "Thank you, little Cordelia." Then he patted my shoulder and drove away.

In the months that followed, Uncle Haskell became a lay physician to Mrs. Eltwing. It happened shortly after the night when she had been lost in our woods that Uncle Haskell and I were riding past the Eltwings' place one evening and found her standing at the gate, her face swollen with crying, her eyes wild, her hair and clothing disarrayed. The housekeeper was trying to coax her to come inside, but whenever the woman tried to touch her, Katy Eltwing screamed and clung to the wooden pickets of the fence. I noticed that Uncle Haskell's face looked pale as we reined our horses and sat for a moment in our saddles watching a scene that was both sorrowful and revolting.

Then Uncle Haskell dismounted and walked over toward the fence where Katy Eltwing stood.

"Mrs. Eltwing," he said pleasantly, "do you remember me? May I come in and talk with you for a few minutes?"

She stared at him for a brief time and then ran to him, her face like that of a child restored to sweetness after a tantrum. He took her hand and the two of them walked slowly into the house, Uncle Haskell talking to her softly, the housekeeper and I following in silent wonder.

When Jonathan Eltwing came home at twilight he found Uncle Haskell at the piano playing a few sim-

ple melodies which he remembered from his youth,
and Mrs. Eltwing sitting beside him, subdued and
apparently content. She held out a hand to her husband when he came toward her.

"The golden haired man came to me when I was
frightened, Jonathan. Please don't let him go away
again."

Jonathan Eltwing may not have liked to do it, but
there were many days when he was forced to call
upon Uncle Haskell for help. And Uncle Haskell, on
his part, may not have liked to have his self-centered
way of life upset. He never, however, refused to go
to Katy Eltwing when she needed him although he
always insisted that either Aunt Cordelia or I go with
him; sometimes it seemed to me that my poised and
self-confident uncle showed signs of being a timorous
boy when he was summoned to the Eltwing home.
He was always tired and silent when his hours of
providing therapy for Katy Eltwing were over.

She wanted him to play for her when her hands,
which had so recently held the high skill of the artist,
now stumbled and faltered over the keys. Uncle
Haskell was not an accomplished musician, but he
was able to play excerpts from the musical plays that
were popular when he and Mrs. Eltwing were young,
as well as the familiar aria from some opera. He had
a pleasant baritone voice, and this compensated in
some measure for the occasional false note he struck
on the keyboard.

She loved to hear him sing *My heart at thy sweet
voice* from *Samson and Delilah;* sometimes she
wanted him to sing it over and over again as a child
wants to hear a story retold time after time. I used to

wonder what Jonathan Eltwing thought about in his
study as he listened to that tender love song sung a
dozen times over while he tried to concentrate upon
the ordeal of Dostoievsky.

The pattern of a lifetime did not change for Uncle
Haskell except for these sessions with Katy Eltwing.
He still had occasion to fill his old golf bag with
empty bottles every so often; he continued to per-
petuate his myth of being a busy writer; he still
clung to his role of a gentleman born to a gracious
way of life. He still was completely ridiculous (that's
if you loved him at all) and completely disgusting
(that's if you were a stranger to that side of him
which was seldom seen).

But as far at his attitude toward Mrs. Eltwing was
concerned, Uncle Haskell was truly the gentleman he
would have liked to be. He was gentle and patient
with her, and he was unfailingly silent about her. He
never discussed her condition even with Aunt Cordelia or me.

There was very little that either Aunt Cordelia or
I could do for the Eltwings; sometimes my aunt prepared little Sunday night suppers for them—strange
supper parties in which Aunt Cordelia did not dare
approach Katy Eltwing, but would sit talking to
Jonathan when the meal was finished while Uncle
Haskell took Mrs. Eltwing for a walk, or sat at the
piano playing for her and singing the songs she
loved. Often she would fall asleep against his shoulder
and he would lift her in his arms, carrying her to the
couch in the library, where her husband would cover
her carefully and sit close beside her. It was like
a strange, unreal play. Sometimes I was happy to

escape to the Trevorts and taste the air of reality again with Danny and his kindly, very normal parents.

As the months passed, we watched Katy Eltwing become feebler, farther and farther removed from everything about her. It was very hard to persuade her to eat enough for the maintenance of her strength. Aunt Cordelia used to cook every nourishing delicacy she could remember, and send me over with covered bowls of food that might tempt Mrs. Eltwing's appetite. Jonathan used to coax his wife to eat whatever I brought over, but after a few spoonfuls, she would turn wearily away, shaking her head.

"She used to enjoy food so much," Jonathan Eltwing told me on one such occasion when we had tried to tempt her into eating. "She enjoyed all good things—good food, beautiful objects, beautiful people. She had a great fondness for gold; every piece of jewelry she selected was of gold. I used to think that the metal pins and necklaces she bought were too heavy for her, but they were what she wanted. And velvet for her dresses—soft velvets and gold. How she loved that combination."

I thought of Uncle Haskell's bright hair and the dark velvet of his smoking jacket on that autumn afternoon when she first saw him. Soft velvet and gold; that combination and with it high praise for the turbulent music that obviously had shaken her as she played it.

As she became weaker, she no longer cared for the songs that previously had given her pleasure. For weeks she lay in her bed, silent and uncomprehending. Uncle Haskell and I went to see her almost daily; then one evening he turned to Jonathan Eltwing as if he had come to a sudden decision. "I can do nothing for her, Jonathan; I will not come here again."

"It is possible that she recognizes you, Haskell," Jonathan began.

Uncle Haskell almost plunged from the room. "No, she doesn't, I'm sure of that. If I could help her, I would, but it's no use. Surely you understand, Jonathan. I have my work—there are many pressures upon me . . ."

It was the first time he had resorted to his lies in connection with anything that had to do with Katy Eltwing.

She died one bright summer morning. When I told Uncle Haskell about it, he turned his head and had nothing to say. He did not go to her funeral.

According to Mrs. Peters there was an old cliché among the men of the neighborhood, the gist of which was the fact that they had never known Haskell Bishop when he wasn't drinking, but neither had they ever known him when he was drunk. He was drunk, however, the day Katy Eltwing was buried, sadly and pathetically drunk. He never spoke of that day afterward, nor did he ever again mention the little woman who had loved him—or who had loved something he represented.

Chapter Eight

Carlotta thought that I was completely bereft of my senses when I chose to live with Aunt Cordelia during my high school years.

"You won't have any dates, Julie; you simply won't. How many high school boys will have a car to drive out into the country, or how many of them—unless you date upperclassmen—are going to be old enough to drive? And anyway, Julie, how many boys are going to want to face Miss Cordelia if they should bring you home five minutes late some night?"

Carlotta was taking a room in town; when she heard that I was staying with Aunt Cordelia, she tried to rent my old room at home, but Father and Alicia would have none of it. "That room is Julie's whenever she wishes to stay in town," they said, and so Carlotta found an even more desirable place with a young couple, neither of whom paid the slightest attention to the whereabouts of their pretty tenant.

For two years while Carlotta sailed from one boy

to another, attended every dance and football game, and shook her head pityingly at me as she realized the fulfillment of her prophesies, I might still have been twelve years old and a student in the old one-room rural school, for all the social life I had. Occasionally Father invited me to a college affair and introduced me to some of the young men in his classes; but young college men were interested in young college women for the most part, and their attentions to me were more or less in the line of duty. And Carlotta had been right about the high school boys: they dated the girls who lived in town. The girls who lived in town constituted an "in-group"; if you lived five miles out in the country and were looked after by an austere aunt—well, you simply were not considered eligible for the "in-group."

I was not too unhappy during those first two years. Danny or Jim Ferris saw to it that I got into town for the football games; Alicia insisted that I try out for dramatics and I had parts in a couple of school plays; there were occasional weekends with Father and Alicia during which I had sophisticated experiences that many of the "in-group" girls might have envied. My existence was hardly that of a recluse.

There were, however, many times when I felt lonely, when I had the aching feeling that life was passing by me and that I was missing something very desirable. Sometimes I leaned on the sill of my window and looked out at the night with a longing that I was not able to define, but one which was responsible for many a sigh and even a few tears.

And then suddenly, there was Brett Kingsman. Suddenly there was a new chapter of my life opening before me. It seemed very beautiful and marvelous, but there were tensions and anxieties arising as suddenly as love had arisen, and I felt bewildered as I tried to face them.

It was Alicia who sharpened those tensions and anxieties for me. She did it indirectly, of course, and without malice. Actually, she set things in motion through an assignment given to her third hour English class where I sat beside the handsome transfer student who had created a sizable furor among the girls, "in-group" as well as outsiders.

My stepmother came to her classes each day beautifully groomed, poised, alert, and with a sweet-sour quality to her comments that made them palatable in spite of an occasional sting. I was quite proud of her, really, although for a long time the memory of Laura's room and of my lonely, bewildered feeling that morning in the breakfast nook tinged my feeling for her ever so slightly. But I couldn't deny the fact that she was a charming person and an exceptionally fine teacher. There was no loafing in Mrs. Trelling's classes; we had to dig ideas out of our own minds instead of reference books; we were treated to no pablum feedings of "true-false" or "fill-in-the-blank" tests. And our themes were not devoted to accounts of a vacation trip or a résumé of *Silas Marner*. Alicia liked originality and independence of thinking; sometimes, however, she had considerable difficulty in discovering either among the adolescents who sat before her.

I remember how fresh and radiant she looked that morning, her blue eyes cool and smiling under her smooth black brows. It occurred to me that my father's wife was still very happy after almost three years, and I envied her a little. I kept telling myself that I was happy, but I wasn't. There was too much anxiety, too many half-hidden uncertainties in my feeling for Brett Kingsman. I had no wish to be as old as Alicia—her forty-odd years seemed quite appalling to me—but I wished for her confidence, her air of what I had recently learned to call *savoir faire*. Uncle Haskell had this quality too, but there was a difference; with Alicia, it was genuine.

I was thinking of these things when I suddenly became aware of her assignment.

"I assume that each of you has read Thoreau's *Civil Disobedience* since it is on the list of required readings—if not, perhaps this assignment will provide motivation for doing so over the weekend." Alicia leaned her elbows on the desk, lacing her slender fingers together and smiling in a way that took the edge off her words. "For next week's assignment I'd like you to write a paper on *Civil Disobedience*, explaining Thoreau's justification of his position and your own reactions to that position." Alicia paid no attention to a slight moan that swept heavenward from the class, and continued serenely. "I will throw out a few points that you might think about in organizing your paper: for example, remembering that *Civil Disobedience* was written in angry protest against the Fugitive Slave Law and the prospect of war with Mexico, what do you think Thoreau's reaction would have been to the secession of the southern states a few years later? And in our own century, how would he have stood with those who violated the 18th amendment? Incidentally, how do you think he would have felt about Federal Aid to Education?"

It was plain that Alicia was enjoying herself. "You may wish to explore the growth of Gandhi's passive resistance struggle in India and its relation to Thoreau's theory. Or again, you might like to discuss in terms of Thoreau's convictions, such a statement as I have placed on the board." She pointed to a sentence which most of us had read idly when we entered the room: "The goal of counseling is to help the individual adjust to his environment."

I commenced jotting down a few notes hurriedly; it was not going to be an easy paper, but I felt a bit of excitement growing in me as I thought of some possibilities for discussion. It was while I was writing that Brett slammed a book down on the arm of his chair, sent a couple pencils rattling to the floor and then leaned back, glaring at Alicia.

She was as smooth as ice cream. "You will have a week to complete your paper. I'd like it typed, please, double-spaced. If any one of you wishes to talk with me about the assignment, you may make an appointment with me during one of my office hours." She flipped a few cards through her fingers as the bell rang, studied the notations briefly and then added, "I should like to see Jim Ferris for a short time at eleven; Norma Grayson at four this afternoon; Julie Trelling at four-fifteen. That is all. You are dismissed."

Out in the corridor Brett got rid of his rage, employing me as a sounding-board. "Lord, how I hate schoolteachers," he railed, "how I hate 'em in general and your highbrow stepmama in particular. What did your old man mean, I wonder, getting himself tied up to that she-encyclopaedia." He turned toward me savagely. "She's out to get me, Julie; she's going to see to it that I flunk English again."

And I, who in former years would have had a biting answer for this sort of attitude, was soft as a mound of mashed potatoes. "I'll help you, Brett; I'm not going to see you flunk, darling."

He pressed my arm a little at that. "I wonder what the old girl wants to see you about, honey?"

I had been wondering about the same thing. "I don't know, Brett; maybe something about my schedule for next year." I could hardly tear myself away at the door of my next class. "Will you meet me outside her office about four-thirty?" I asked.

"I don't know, Julie, baby; I will if I can. Anyway, I'll give you a ring sometime this evening." He slipped his arm around me for a second, and Danny Trevort, who was coming down the hall toward us, gave me a disgusted look. "How are you, Julie, *baby?*" he hissed, as we walked into class together.

How Danny knew it, I don't know for I had never discussed it with him, but it was true that Brett's pet names for me sometimes sent a shiver of distaste down my spine. I had lived with Aunt Cordelia too long to enjoy being called "Julie, baby" or "Honeybun" or "Sugar." They were foolish in the first place and rather revoltingly sticky for someone who was strictly a high protein girl. Still, it was Brett who gave me those names and Brett was the boy whom I called "my beloved" in the secrecy of my own dreams. When one loves, one must learn to adjust, to be understanding, I thought.

There had been moments when I very nearly forgot that bit of wisdom; moments like the ones when we sat together in the darkened theater over at the college and watched a famous pair of actors in *Macbeth*. I remember sitting tense as the door to King Duncan's bedroom opened and Lady Macbeth came out leaning against the wall for support, looking in horror at her blood-drenched hands. I pressed Brett's arm in my excitement, but he did not share my mood. He yawned overtly and leaned his cheek down to mine. "Are you bored too, honey?" he asked hopefully.

I felt strongly out of tune with Brett that night after the play, and he noticed it.

"The whole thing was a lot of hogwash as far as I'm concerned," he said belligerently as we left the theater.

"It has done pretty well for the past three centuries in spite of your opinion," I said sharply, the Aunt Cordelia-influence getting the upper hand of me.

Brett dropped my hand abruptly. "Well, you can have it, schoolmarm," he said, and the contempt in his voice was unmistakable.

Our romance trembled in the air for a while that evening, but it soon became steady again, for I was not long in feeling contritely apologetic for my sharpness, and Brett, who was in immediate need of help with an English assignment, was sweetly forgiving. We reassured one another of our love, and I told myself that I must expect to make adjustments to Brett's tastes. Wasn't that what love was all about— a mutual understanding, a give-and-take relationship? I didn't like it when a small thought intruded itself, suggesting that so far, our understanding was hardly mutual, and that up to the present, I was doing all the giving and Brett was doing the taking.

At any rate, I was not going to risk losing Brett because I had learned to enjoy Shakespeare and he hadn't. Never, I thought, for Brett was a shining wonder to which I could never quite grow accustomed. He was tall, wide of shoulder and narrow of hip, beautifully bronzed. His eyes were blue and heavily lashed, his black hair slightly wavy, his square chin cleft. There was just one feature of Brett's handsome face that I found to be not quite perfect: his mouth was too soft looking, too loose. That was all; and I felt that I was being far too critical in noticing that one defect at all. Almost all the girls in school had been dazzled by him when he entered as a transfer student early in the year, and wonder of wonders, of all the girls he had chosen Julie Trelling. Carlotta was deeply impressed; she remembered after a long lapse that she and I had been close friends since we were little seven-year-olds.

Aunt Cordelia had no comment to make upon my Brett other than the fact that he was, indeed, handsome. She asked me a few questions about him—he had trouble with English, she knew, but that was not uncommon; some of her most intelligent boys had faltered before noun clauses and Shakespearean sonnets. Brett was, no doubt, more inclined toward mathematics or science? No? Music or art, perhaps? Athletics? When I had to admit that Brett had no talent or inclination in any of these areas, Aunt Cordelia only raised her brows expressively.

I wanted to say, "What about your own brother" but with the thought I realized that I was admitting a likeness between Brett and Uncle Haskell. It was not an admission that pleased me; neither was the fact that Uncle Haskell was the one older person in my family for whom Brett had expressed an interest.

"Fine old boy—I really like him," Brett told me with some admiration after listening for an hour to Uncle Haskell's empty boasting.

Being in love with Brett was not pure joy. I

thought about it that afternoon on the Thoreau assignment day as I walked down the corridor in the Administration Building and seated myself outside Alicia's office. The nameplate on her door said simply "Mrs. A. Trelling"; it seemed rather nice, I thought, that Alicia and I had the same name. I never could quite get used to it. In my early months of high school I used to go inside her office and say, "Good morning, Mrs. Trelling," and she would grin at me and say "Try 'Alicia' when we're in here alone, Julie; it's much friendlier."

I smiled to myself as I thought of the relatives who had been my teachers; I supposed there would be Father in the future, possibly Bill.

We were a schoolteacherish family, there was no doubt of that. But we were a nice family; I liked us. Father and Alicia had been very fine about my deciding to live with Aunt Cordelia; they had looked at me a bit thoughtfully when I told them as gracefully as I could that somehow the big house among the trees had come to seem like home to me, and they nodded although they may have felt some doubt when I added a bit of embroidery to my decision by implying that Aunt Cordelia was hardly able to face my leaving her. But they had neither remonstrated nor pled; they told me that their home was mine, come homesickness, a bad storm, a hankering for a holiday or a complete change of mind. And thus we had left it. We three had been very good friends; in some ways having Alicia was a little like having Laura again. She used to call and ask me if I'd do her hair for a special occasion, and we would chat by the hour as I tried to achieve the effect she particularly liked. Sometimes I would see Father smiling above the book he was reading, and I knew that he was pleased at the friendship between Alicia and me.

They were younger and gayer than Aunt Cordelia, of course, and could offer me many advantages that she could not. If there was a special concert or play to be given over at the college, there was always an invitation for me to stay in town and accompany them. Sometimes they invited Danny Trevort too, not that Danny was anything more to me than the kid I'd grown up with, but they liked him and the four of us had had great fun together. They even took Danny and me to New York once, picking Chris up on the way, and we had gone on a dozen or more interesting forays into the big city, having the gay and carefree kind of vacation that none of us would ever forget.

All that had been before Brett. They didn't invite Danny with me any longer, because he and I had become virtually enemies, but they didn't invite Brett either. And the more coolness they showed toward Brett, the more I saw him as being wronged and misunderstood; therefore the more I was determined to stand by him.

Norma Grayson emerged from Alicia's office at last, looking weary but triumphant. "You're to go in now," she said, nodding toward the door. Then she laid her hand on my arm. "She was real nice, Julie; she went through that *Civil Disobedience* thing for me, and I think that I halfway understand what the guy was talking about. It's pretty ghastly, though, isn't it?"

The whole world seemed a little ghastly to me that afternoon. I said, "It certainly is," to Norma, and then went into the office and took a chair beside Alicia's desk. She looked a little worn, too, I thought.

"How are you, Miss Julie Trelling?" she asked, smiling at me. "You haven't quite seemed yourself lately; I've been concerned about you."

"I'm perfectly well, Alicia, really," I said and settled myself to hear whatever she had to say.

"Good. I suppose it's the end-of-the-year pressure that's moving in on all of us, isn't it? Well, first of all, there's the concert at Collins Hall next week. Your father and I wondered if you would stay in and go with us Saturday evening. You know Ted Bolling, the young assistant in your father's office? He's going as our guest, and he very definitely brightened up when I suggested that you might be able to come along."

I stiffened. Saturday night. They knew I'd have a date with Brett on Saturday night, and they were deliberately trying to hurt him by getting me out with someone else. I wanted to hear that concert; I'd wanted to hear it for weeks, and there was nothing particularly wrong with Ted Bolling, except that he wasn't Brett Kingsman. But I was not going to be sucked in by intrigue.

"I'm sorry, Alicia, but I can't possibly. I always have a date with Brett on Saturday night. I thought that you and Father knew that."

Alicia's brows moved ever so slightly. "Oh, yes, of course. Well, your father will be sorry; he had been looking forward to seeing you. You haven't been over to talk with him lately."

I didn't say anything, and for just a few seconds there was silence between us. Then Alicia opened a drawer, took out a sheaf of papers and said briskly —artificially, I thought—"Apropos of Brett, I have a number of his papers here, Julie. The later ones have shown quite a lot of improvement over his earlier work; however, it's rather an erratic improvement. What I mean is that there will be an intelligently stated idea in one paragraph followed by a meaningless string of words that Brett seems to feel I'll recognize as a sentence. Would you have a theory concerning this discrepancy in quality?"

I knew what was coming. I hadn't meant to do another person's work for him at first, but Brett had a way with him, and week after week his papers had become more and more nearly complete copies of my dictation. I had never cheated before, and I was hard put to rationalize the whole sorry business. It helped to remember that Laura had once said that it was a privilege for her to be able to help Bill with his thesis; now, I tried to tell myself, I could understand exactly how she felt. But my message didn't quite ring true; in my heart I knew there was a difference between Laura's situation and mine. After all, she had only *helped* Bill.

It had all commenced quite early in the year. The first time Brett ever noticed me had been one day in class when papers were being returned to us. He had smiled at me rather sourly and asked, "Are you really that good or do you get this kind of grade because her highness is your stepmother?"

I hadn't liked that much, but I just said, "I think it's because I happen to like English. I don't always make such grades in math."

He looked friendlier. "Well, congratulations, sugar. You're pretty smooth, no matter what kind of grades you make."

When we were dismissed that day, Brett walked close behind me. Out in the hall he said, "Look, baby, how about giving me a hand with this paper? The old girl says I have to correct and return it by to-morrow—" He unfolded a paper that was plastered with red code signs made by Alicia's pencil.

I said, "Of course, Brett, I'll be glad to help you." And that is the way the relationship which I thought of as a romance had started. A lot of very popular girls in high school thought of it as a romance too, and I was suddenly the object of their envy. I hadn't been particularly envied before; I had been simply a little grind who lived out in the country and who made good grades because a grim old aunt saw to it that every scrap of homework was completed and turned in. Brett Kingsman's attentions had changed that picture in their minds.

But I had become worried about the help I was giving him. "This is the idea, Brett; now put it into your own words, just as simply and clearly as you can," I'd tell him. And then I'd get a kiss, a compliment or two, and finally a plea that was almost a command: "Now, what was that again, sugar? How did you say it just now?"

Alicia was speaking again. "I have read your papers for quite a long time, Julie, and I recognize your style of writing, your approach to ideas. What I find here are papers done by you with a few semiliterate lines contributed by Brett. It's a bit on the shabby side, isn't it?"

I was close to tears, but I forced them back and tried to summon strength for a counterattack. "I've only been trying to give him a lift, Alicia. Your course *is* difficult, and Brett has lost so much schooling because of his family moving oround from place to place. Anyway, everybody is against him. You know that neither you nor Father can stand the sight of him."

Alicia squared her shoulders, and there was really an air of Aunt Cordelia about her. "Julie, any person in my classes is welcome to come into this office to discuss his difficulties. Any person who takes the trouble to read assigned material, who makes any effort on his own to discover a few ideas and arrange them—that student can depend upon my help whether I like him or not. Kingsman hasn't made the slightest effort. He is sullen, lazy, smart-alecky and dishonest." She paused a minute and looked at me steadily. "What in Heavens' name do you mean by getting involved with this boy, Julie?"

All the fire that I withheld from Brett was ready for Alicia. "You wouldn't know, would you, Alicia? You have Father just as Laura has Bill. You have someone to love you and a home where you feel secure, and you don't have to be lonely and not sure where you really belong. Well, I'm not so lucky as you. I need love very much, and when I find someone who gives it to me, I'm going to hold on to him —and you can tell Father that—and Laura—and everybody."

I was half-crying, half-shouting at her; even in my overwrought state I noticed that she looked pale. It was a rough session for both of us.

"Julie, believe me, I am not unsympathetic. I know what it means to be lonely, and I know that insecurity is frightening. But you never gain security by selling out for a shoddy something that only resembles love."

"You're saying then, that Brett is shoddy?"

"I think that he is very immature and that he is

using you for his own purposes. He is giving you nothing and taking all he can get. He may change some day; I doubt it, but he may. Until he does, yes, he's shoddy."

"Not in the same class with Father or Bill or—or—"

"That's right. Or Dan Trevort or Chris or Ted Bolling. Or a dozen others I could name for you."

I got up with what I felt was considerable dignity. "Well, Alicia, I'll say just this: I don't care whether you or Father or Laura or any of the people you've named like Brett or not. I love him, and I'm going to stand by him."

Alicia also got up with dignity. "Very well, Julie. That is your right. But understand this: if any more papers done by Julie Trelling are handed in by Brett Kingsman, you are both going to the Dean's office. Brett will flunk the course, and you will be disciplined as the Dean sees fit. You had just as well begin learning what Brett is going to mean for you."

I walked out of the office without looking at her. It didn't seem possible that we had ever been friends.

Brett wasn't there to drive me home; neither was Danny, who probably had thought that I was staying in town when I hadn't shown up at our usual meeting place for the drive home. I could have asked Father to take me home or I could have called Aunt Cordelia, or have waited an hour for the next bus, but the spirit of martyrdom was strong upon me and I decided to walk the five miles home. I rather hoped that they'd find me along the wayside sometime before dawn, perhaps, in a state of complete exhaustion.

I'd only walked a little over a mile, however, when a car came tearing down the dusty road toward me. It made a U turn a few yards in front of me and then stopped at the side of the road. A very grim-looking Danny sat behind the wheel and watched me approach.

"You could have told me your plans, Julie," he said angrily. "How was I to know that you didn't have a way to get home? Couldn't gorgeous Kingsman afford the gas to drive you out or is he having his beauty-nap?"

"I wasn't with Brett in the first place, and I'm under no compulsion to tell you my plans in the second place. I don't know why you've come out here to meet me; I'm nothing to you."

Danny was pretty furious. He said, "You've just made the most doggoned accurate statement that I've heard in days. You are absolutely nothing to me. Absolutely. But you're wrong about my coming out to meet you. It's just a coincidence—even now I have half a mind to make you walk the rest of the way—" He jerked the car door open. "Get in," he barked at me and I did, ungraciously accepting his favor while I remembered with satisfaction that I had once blacked his eye.

The world was against me that evening. Alicia was mad. Danny was mad. Aunt Cordelia was irked because I hadn't told Danny that I was staying after school, thus causing him to make another trip. I told her that he had not come back to meet me, that he was going into town for some other reason—he hadn't told me what—but she said, nonsense, that he'd called to find out if I was home and a few minutes later had started down the road.

I went up to my room and tried to think of what it would be like when Brett and I were married; I thought about how I would inform my entire family that be it Thanksgiving or Christmas or any other holiday, if Brett were not welcome, then they could count upon it, Julie would not be on hand either. I thought of how I'd stand by him and comfort him with my love and loyalty. But try as I would, I couldn't get Brett to emerge in my day-dream as a wronged but valiant and heroic figure; I kept seeing him behave like a sullen child in spite of all my efforts.

It was getting late when Brett finally called to ask if he could come out for a while and talk over our English assignment. He sounded sleepy and morose; I thought of what Danny had said about his having a beauty-nap, but I pushed the thought aside and told him joyfully that yes, he might come out. Aunt Cordelia, who sat beside the table reading, said, "Until ten, Julia; no later." She didn't lift her eyes from her book.

Brett and I sat in the living room and talked; Aunt Cordelia did not come in to meet him. If it had been Danny who was calling on me, there would have been a pleasant welcome for him and some sort of refreshment. Not for Brett. She remained seated with her book at hand, her knees crossed, and her foot swinging back and forth with what appeared to be mild agitation after some of Brett's remarks.

He wanted help, of course, with the paper on *Civil Disobedience*. He had a notebook ready and his pen poised above it. "Tell me how to begin it, sugar," he said wearily, knowing, I suspect, that it was going to be tiresome business in getting a clear dictation from me and then expending precious energy in putting my words down on paper.

"I can't tell you what to say, Brett; I just can't do that. Why don't you write in your own words just why you think Thoreau felt that a man is justified at times in not paying his taxes, in not fighting for a cause in which he—"

Brett slammed his notebook shut. "How am I going to say it in my own words? I haven't read the stupid thing, and I have no intention of reading it. If you don't want to help me, just say so."

I thought that foot beside the dining room table was going to fly through the door. Even my love cracked a little.

"Well, I can't do your paper for you, Brett, if that's what you mean. I've been doing too much as it is. We're going to get in trouble, both of us; Alicia told me so this afternoon." Let Aunt Cordelia hear it, I thought; I supposed that it was just as well.

There wasn't any love in Brett's eyes as he sat staring at me. Finally he said, "So that's it, is it? You're afraid of getting your own neck in the noose. It's all right if I flunk English again, but you're not going to get in bad with your precious stepma. Lord, how I hate schoolteachers," he said, for the second time within twelve hours.

We sat for a while in silence, and Aunt Cordelia's foot quieted down as if it were waiting. I was so mad at that point that I was ready to tell Brett that our romance was over. But Brett changed his tactics suddenly and swept down my defenses.

He said, "I'm sorry, honey. Forget the whole lousy business. I might just as well flunk English again, because it's a sure thing that math is down the drain." He shrugged, and taking both my hands, drew me to my feet. "Don't be mad, little sugar; come out to the car and say good night," he whispered.

He was so handsome, so masterful looking with his height and his beautifully wide shoulders. I com-

menced to melt in the warmth of his sudden tenderness. We went down the long path toward his car,
Brett's arm around my waist, his cheek resting against
my hair. When we reached the end of the path he
said, "Let's go for just a little walk, honey; just a
few minutes together."

"I can't, Brett—it's getting late. I simply can't. Aunt
Cordelia will—"

There was another flash of anger. "Look, Julie, are
you letting that old woman run your life? If you are,
you can count me out. I'm not coming out here to
be told that you can't help me out of a tight spot,
you can't take a little walk in the woods, you can't
do anything. I thought you loved me, but if you
don't, all right, say so. I'll begin looking around
somewhere else."

The next minute we were walking back into the
woods—just a short, little walk to show that I loved
him.

It was a wonderful night; the world looked as if
it had been dipped in some liquid silver poured out
of the moon. The woods were so still and radiant
that it brought a catch of wistfulness to my throat.
Such beauty ought not to be wasted in small talk.
I thought of Jessica and young Lorenzo watching
that moon together, matching their flashes of imagery,
fitting them together into a perfect mosaic of poetry:

"The moon shines bright: in such a night as this
When the sweet wind did gently kiss the trees
And they did make no noise; in such a night
Troilus methinks mounted the Trojan walls
And sighed his soul toward the Grecian tents,
Where Cressid lay that night."

I wished that Brett would say those lines to me as
we walked in the moonlight, and that I could then
say:

> "In such a night
> Did Thisbe fearfully o'ertrip the dew,
> And saw the lion's shadow ere himself
> And ran dismay'd away."

I felt a longing for Brett to understanding my feelings, for an affinity between us such as must have
existed between Jessica and young Lorenzo that radiant night.

But Brett had not read much of Shakespeare, and
even if he had known every play and every sonnet by
rote, he would not have been at that moment in a
mood to quote any of the immortal lines. His arms
were suddenly holding me very tightly. "I love you
so much, little honey-bun, little sugar—" I didn't much
care for the pet names, but that night he could have
run down the entire dessert menu of a well-stocked
restaurant and I wouldn't have objected.

We stood close in one another's arms and Brett
was whispering, "You understand, don't you, sugar,
don't you, Julie, baby—?"

Julie, baby, was indeed beginning to understand.
The word was beginning to come through clearly to
her, and Shakespeare was fading away into the background like muted music contrasting with the tumult
of a mighty drama.

Then, as if on cue, there emerged from left wing a
dapper, slender figure which advanced airily to center
stage, laid aside an ancient golf bag, and extended a
cordial hand toward the leading man.

"Kingsman, dear boy, what luck to have run across you," Uncle Haskell exclaimed gaily. He immediately pretended to be chagrined at having burst in upon us, but I knew Uncle Haskell; he did not know the meaning of chagrin.

"So awfully sorry to have intruded upon a tender moment, children," he said playfully. "Still, it's my good fortune to have found you, Brett. Do you know that you were the subject of a telephone conversation between me and one of the best known producers in New York not more than two hours ago?"

Brett was staring at Uncle Haskell a little stupidly, but I could see that his interest was beginning to come through the fog. He liked Uncle Haskell; he wouldn't for very long, but that night my uncle seemed to be opening up new vistas for Brett.

Uncle Haskell disposed of me in a hurry. "Julie, my pet, I think you'd better run along now. Brett can tell you his good news tomorrow. I have an idea that Aunt Cordelia would like you safe inside. Ten o'clock comes on apace, you know."

I felt weak and ill with humiliation, anger, anxiety, and uncertainty. I lingered a few yards away and listened for a minute or two while Uncle Haskell unfolded his story. He would never have considered merely sending an amorous young man on his way and giving an amorous young niece a brief bedtime lecture. Uncle Haskell's soul would have revolted at the image of himself as an upholder of morals; he preferred to achieve the same result by means less hackneyed. Thus, his story that a producer in New York, beside himself with joy in producing Uncle Haskell's play, had telephoned to ask about a prospect for a part—"a minor part, mind you, but not an unimportant one—" My uncle was pouring the soothing unguent on Brett's bruised feelings. Brett, of course, was young and inexperienced; still, Uncle Haskell had told E.J. that this young fellow was extraordinarily handsome, had a natural grace and flair for the dramatic—

I had heard enough. That Brett was weak, I had to admit, but he didn't deserve cruelty like this. I ran through the woods and up the steps to the old porch swing where Aunt Cordelia was waiting for me.

I expected a lecture, but she was strangely quiet. Let me forget to dust the living room or mend a torn blouse, and she would hold forth at length; let me run off into the woods with Brett Kingsman, and she had nothing to say. Finally, when she didn't speak, I said, "I'm sorry, Aunt Cordelia; I shouldn't have gone out there tonight."

She put her hand on mine for a second; that was all, just the faintest pressure on my hand. After that we sat in silence.

We heard Brett's car roar down the road after a while; then later, a long time later, we heard Uncle Haskell emerging from the woods, his pleasant voice humming, *My heart at thy sweet voice*, and I wondered if he were deliberately hurting himself by remembering that aria which Katy Eltwing had loved to hear him sing. He seemed cheerful enough, however, when he glimpsed us among the shadows and waved to us.

"Good night, my girls," he called, and strode away toward his carriage-house apartment.

"You sent him out there for me, didn't you, Aunt Cordelia?" I asked after a while.

"He went of his own accord," she said quietly. "I

was frightened tonight, Julia. For the first time that
I can remember, I gave way to panic. Then I called
Haskell. I guess you realize that he has never in his
life lifted a burden from me; that is why your father
and Jonathan have disliked him so much. But tonight, he did. He treated me the way a strong brother
treats a sister when she is weak."

Upstairs in my room I stood at the window and
looked out at the silver world.

"On such a night," I thought, "were ill and good,
Bright and unlovely; precious, tawdry,
All mingled into one
And pressed against my heart."

It was a long way from Shakespeare, but it gave me
a bit of comfort to think in blank verse at the close
of a particularly wretched day.

Chapter Nine

That spring which marked the end of my junior year
in high school was a difficult one for me. When Brett
had the hard news straight from Uncle Haskell that
E. J. had felt the academic record of Bishop's protegé
made an interview unnecessary, Brett was through
with me, my family, and any person who had a kind
word for any one of us. He immediately began taking
Carlotta Berry to all the spring activities at school
whereupon Carlotta glowed and began regarding me
as if I were a country cousin. Even Danny refused
to let bygones be bygones, and he invited Eden
Brownlee to go to the prom with him when he knew
that I had no choice but to stay at home. Ted Bolling,
who, Alicia said, had brightened at the mention of
my name, had in the meantime brightened at the
presence of a young secretary from the English department. I was a social outcast as suddenly as I had
become the envy of half the girls in school when
Brett first paid attention to me.

The loneliness and sense of loss left an aching void inside me, and the knowledge that everyone knew I had been jilted was an added stroke of bitterness. I chose not to remember Brett's inadequacies; but to dwell upon his attractiveness, his moments of tenderness; there were many sweet memories, and they made the bitterness of Carlotta's taking over everything that had belonged to me very hard to bear.

I wrote a little poetry as a release, and it helped somewhat, although even in my misery, I knew that it was not very good poetry. I grew apathetic about my schoolwork and did a C paper on *Civil Disobedience* for Alicia, who made no comment, but shook her head ever so slightly when she handed it back to me. It was a pity; I had intended writing a really superior paper for her on that day when she made the assignment.

From my window I watched the full moon—a moon that reminded me of Brett—become shadowed, little by little until there was only a deep blackness in the woods at night. I would sit there wakeful, hour after hour, and wonder if this aching around my heart, this sense of being alone, forlorn and unwanted in a world where there was gayety and love for others of my age, was going to continue for all of my days.

Everyone in my family was kind to me that spring. Father came out and took me for long drives; Alicia gave me a crisp, white suit with a coral blouse that would have sent me into raptures ordinarily; Laura wrote that she and my small namesake were looking forward to visiting me in August. And Aunt Cordelia was wonderful. There was not one sermon or high and mighty word from her. I think that I began to love Aunt Cordelia that spring.

Day followed day, each heavier than the other, for six weeks or so, and then the miracle happened. I have often thought about that miracle: surely the weight under which I had labored had gradually been lessening and the miracle was not a miracle at all. I think not though; it still seems like a miracle and this is how it was:

I had gone to sleep in sorrow and longing; I awoke the next morning—and something had happened. It was a bright summer morning and every leaf on the trees outside seemed to have been polished, glittering as they were in the sunlight. The white curtains at my window moved just a little at the touch of the breeze that drifted inside, and my room somehow became a vivid picture to me as if I had pulled aside some veil of indifference and was suddenly aware of it. The walls were as pale as they could get and still be called yellow; the surface of the old walnut bureau and bookcase that Aunt Cordelia and I had refinished was deep with lights which were absorbed in its brown depths. There were white throw rugs on the floor—white rugs that Aunt Cordelia had allowed me to have against the judgment of her practical mind—and there was the small rockingchair upholstered in worn velvet which had been hers when she was a girl. On my desk stood a framed photograph which my aunt had allowed me to keep, the photograph of a lovely young girl smiling at the thought of Jonathan Eltwing, and of a blond young man standing in a studied pose, and a little girl who looked like Laura, laughing at the camera that photographed her.

All these things I saw in that moment of awaking; it wasn't until seconds later that I realized how I

was lying, cool and relaxed in my bed, with a sense
of serenity and quiet happiness enveloping me. I
made myself think of Brett as one might touch an old
wound to determine whether or not it is healed, and
the thought of him miraculously did not hurt. I was
neither angry nor contemptuous; I just remembered
a beautiful boy I had once loved and it was as if something inside me said, "Well, wasn't that lovely? And
now, shall we think of other things?"

For a while I was almost afraid to move, fearful
that just starting the ordinary duties of another day
would break the spell that had descended upon me.
Then I stepped carefully out of bed, and stood in
front of the window breathing deeply. All was well.
Still only a sense of well-being within me. After a
moment I ran into the bathroom, turned on a cold
shower and exulted while the cold lines of water
pelted my body. As I stood glowing after I had
rubbed myself with a big bath towel, I wondered
why so much had been written about love's pain and
so little about the glorious relief of being delivered
from love's pain. I regretted that I did not have
more talent for expressing myself in poetry; I did
resolve, however, that I'd do another paper on *Civil
Disobedience*—it was too late for credit, of course,
but it would give me a chance to show Alicia my real
ability.

I brushed my hair furiously for a good five minutes
and tied it back with a strip of rose velvet. I had a
new housecoat, a gift from Laura, too beautiful for
ordinary occasions, being all of white eyelet cotton
over a lining of petal pink dimity, but I put it on
recklessly and stood before my mirror in unabashed
self-approval. I had sparkle that morning, sparkle that

originated somewhere deep inside me and spread outward to my cheeks and eyes, even it seemed, to the gleam of my hair.

Down in the kitchen Aunt Cordelia was preparing breakfast; the aroma of coffee and Canadian bacon and hot, buttered toast met me as I ran downstairs, and I, who for weeks had been growing thinner as I picked indifferently at my food, was suddenly famished and eager.

We often ate our breakfast in a sunny corner of the kitchen, and Aunt Cordelia had placed two blue bowls on the table, two of Grandmother Bishop's best china bowls, and they were filled with raspberries picked only that morning and still frosted with dew. I was especially perceptive to all things beautiful that morning—raspberries in blue china bowls were enough to make the heart sing.

Aunt Cordelia glanced up from her work as I entered the fragrant kitchen, and I saw a light come into her eyes. She liked seeing me carefully dressed of a morning; she was relieved too, I am sure, to see that I had emerged from the despondency that had weighed upon me for weeks. I smiled at her and hurried to pour the coffee.

"Aunt Cordelia," I said in the tones of a Biblical proclamation, "I have been visited by a miracle."

The light in her eyes was clouded instantly, whether in concern over my sanity or recognition of the fact that miracles could sometimes be embarrassing to a family. She let a circle of pink bacon fall back into the frying pan, and stood looking at me. I laughed at her expression and poured the coffee so recklessly that it overflowed one cup and filled the saucer.

"There are miracles and miracles, Aunt Cordelia;

this one has just given me a new outlook on life. I
went to sleep last night still feeling hurt over Brett;
this morning I am completely free of him. He no
longer matters. It's all over."

She was relieved, there was no doubt about that,
but she took her place at the table as sedately as always. "Love is not love which alters," she quoted as
she passed a basket of toast to me, "when it alteration
finds."

I knew then that she was happy. Aunt Cordelia was
likely to be in one of her better moods when she felt
like quoting Shakespeare.

As we sat together at breakfast that morning I
thought that food had never before tasted so wonderful.

"You know, Aunt Cordelia, there will come a time
when I'll eat berries like these some morning, fresh,
dewy berries like these, and I'll think, 'What's the
matter? These are not like the ones I ate with so
much pleasure long ago.' And then I'll tell myself,
'Of course not, for where is the sunny kitchen overlooking the woods, and where is the beautiful room
upstairs where you awakened that morning, where is
the aunt who quoted from one of Shakespeare's sonnets and above all, where is the sixteen-year-old girl
who had just experienced a miracle?' It will never be
the same, Aunt Cordelia; I'll never eat raspberries like
these again."

Aunt Cordelia just smiled gently. "Maybe not," she
said.

I changed into my blue jeans after breakfast. The
first evidence that things were getting back to normal
was Aunt Cordelia's sharp, "Not in that beautiful
housecoat, Julia," when I commenced to gather up

the dishes. All that morning I worked in a near frenzy of housewifely enthusiasm, polishing furniture, dusting rows of books, washing windows, arranging flowers. Everything I did was a delight; it was a beautiful morning, and I was free of Brett Kingsman!

When I had the house shining, I called Alicia, who got a little bit into my mood of euphoria when I told her all about recent developments. Alicia and I hadn't talked for a long time, but that morning we ignored the coldness that had been between us. "Julie, I'm so happy I could shout," she told me, and we laughed and chatted like two girls again. Later I wrote a long letter to Chris and then one to Laura in which I enclosed a little story for young Julie with crazy drawings which I knew she would like. It was as if I had been away from my family for a long time, and communicating with them again was a great satisfaction.

After supper that night I saddled Peter the Great, and rode down through the woods to the road that led south of our place and which, incidentally, went past Danny Trevort's home. I saw Danny out in the yard striding behind a noisy lawn mower as I approached; he had grown very tall, and I smiled to myself because I could remember a good many years in school when I had been as tall as he was although he was almost two years older. Then suddenly, he had shot up, leaving me far below; it had seemed very strange for quite a while. His hair, that used to be so yellow when we were younger, had grown much darker except where it was bleached by the sun and there was a taut, well-knit look about him that suggested strength in spite of his slenderness. I waved casually as I passed and he gave me a nod; I wasn't too much surprised, however, when some minutes later I heard the pound of his horse's hooves as he rode to overtake me.

We had often raced when we were kids and that night I spurred Peter the Great, urging him to forget his years and give Danny's younger mount a run for his money. We pounded down the hard-packed road, and I felt exhilarated and joyful with the strength and the gallant effort of old Peter as he strove to do me proud.

Finally, Danny drew rein and called to me; after a minute or two we were trotting quietly, side by side.

"You ride too hard, Julie. You'll break your neck one of these days," Danny said. His eyes were friendly and he laughed at the way strands of hair had blown across my face and into my eyes.

"I don't suppose I could have grown up without you and Chris to advise me," I said.

"We did seem to have more sense," he agreed amiably. "You were always one to fly apart in all directions."

"You were both Aunt Cordelia's pets—you know that well enough. Two big, disgusting pets, just because you were male."

"Not at all. She just recognized a certain quality of integrity and maturity of judgment in old Chris and me. You could hardly blame her for that."

"Oh, slurp, slurp, Trevort, I can't stand it," I cried, getting Peter the Great into action again, and we were off, laughing and pounding down the road like two kids gone berserk.

It was fun being with Danny again; it had been a long time since we had been friendly, a whole school year, in fact. Ever since I had started going around with Brett. I had never thought of how Danny might fit into the role of sweetheart; he hadn't seemed to care much about girls until very lately. I knew that he had taken Carlotta to a school dance one night; she had giggled and told me that Danny hadn't so much as held her hand on the way home, no good-night kiss, no more romance about him than when we had been grade school kids under Aunt Cordelia's watchful eye. But he had taken very pretty and popular Eden Brownlee to the prom only a few weeks before, and I had heard no criticism of his behavior from her. It stung me just a little to think of Eden. I believe that I had always considered that Danny was my special property if I wanted to claim him. I had a note up in my leather box of secret treasures, a note from Danny which I had received when I was about nine. It read, "I have for many, many years always thought that you was the nicest girl in school. I will always love you till deth us do part. Yours truly, Danny Trevort." With a document like that in my possession I couldn't help but feel that I had certain rights, and I had rather wanted to claim them that lonely night of the junior prom.

"How are you and Kingsman doing these days?" he asked, when we had quieted down a bit. There was no apparent reason for his asking the question; everybody in school knew how Kingsman and I were doing. However, I was somehow glad to tell him.

"A broken melody," I said, "a shattered remnant of the past."

"Your guardian angel must have been on duty," Danny commented.

I didn't answer. I thought to myself, "No, but there *was* Uncle Haskell."

"How about you and Eden Brownlee?" I asked. I was conscious of what I rather hoped he would say.

But he didn't say it. He looked thoughtful for a minute, and then he said, "She's a right sort of girl. I like her; I guess I like her very much."

So that was that. "Deth" hadn't parted us, but Brett Kingsman had driven quite a wedge between us, and now it looked as if Eden Brownlee were going to finish the job. Danny and I were going to enjoy one of those beautiful brother-sister relationships that summer. Maybe not even that. Not if the Eden Brownlee influence became too potent.

Chris came home for a visit that summer; he, like Danny, was ready for college and a bit patronizing toward me who still had another year in high school. But it was wonderful having him home. We rode and swam, played tennis and went dancing with Danny and Eden. I had never felt so happy and relaxed; I even came to like Eden after a while. After all, it was not her fault that I had lost Danny.

Later in the summer there came Laura and Bill and little Julie; then Father and Alicia joined us and for two joyful weeks Aunt Cordelia and I had our family around us. Jonathan Eltwing often came over for the evening, and occasionally Uncle Haskell risked the failure in meeting a deadline in order to be with us. All the rooms upstairs, so long empty, were filled with people very dear to me. Sometimes I would stand in my own room listening to the buzz of talking and laughter, and I would think of how much life had changed since the October day when I had been brought out to Aunt Cordelia's place under the influence of the doctor's sedative.

Young Julie was my roommate during those two

weeks, little Julie, all dimples and rosy curves, but with what seemed to me a reflective wisdom in her large eyes. She followed me around with a devotion I had never known before, and at night she lay beside me, begging for more stories until she grew sleepy.

"It's a Laura and Julie relationship all over again," I heard Father tell Aunt Cordelia. I recognized it too, never so poignantly as on the night when she breathed a long sigh of delight over the end of a story.

"We're always going to be like this, aren't we, Julie? We're always going to be two Julies together in your room when I come here, aren't we?"

My heart got out of rhythm for a second as I remembered things long past. "For quite a while, Julie; perhaps not always, but for a long time," I whispered.

"Till you marry a big boy and go away?" she asked.

"I'm not going to marry anyone for a long time, Julie."

"Grandpa and Alicia wish that Danny was your boy friend," the small gossip continued.

I laughed. "I don't think there's any chance of that, sweetheart; Danny has another girl."

"Well, I don't want you to have a boy friend and get married. I want you to stay right here so we can always be two Julies together in this room when I come to see you."

Then the summer was over, and the sweet, sad days of autumn moved in once again. Fun was over, and another year of work had commenced. I didn't see Danny and Eden so often after Chris went back to school; Danny still came over to do any heavy work for Aunt Cordelia, putting up storm windows one week, cutting down a tree that leaned too near the electric power line another time. I felt that since he and Eden entered college he treated me as if I were a somewhat dull younger sister. I often sat at my window during the nights of early fall that year, and it seemed to me quite likely that I would, indeed, stay right on being another Julie in the same old room when my little niece came to visit me.

There was another matter that made the autumn days sadder than usual that fall. It was the talk about Carlotta and Brett Kingsman, gossip that everybody seemed to know about before I did. Danny was the one who told me.

He still drove from his home into town where he attended college, and as in other years, I rode with him, sitting in the front seat at his side while the younger freshmen and sophomores were packed in the back. One evening when he had delivered the others at their homes he turned to me suddenly.

"Do you ever see Kingsman these days, Julie?"

"Not if either of us can avoid it," I answered.

"Well, don't. He's no good. There's talk all over town about him and little Lottie. She may be a dumb kid—all right, so she is—but she's far too good for him. And if I ever hear of your being with him, I'll tell Miss Cordelia things that will make her lock you up and—"

"Don't you think, Mr. Trevort, that you're being—"

"Shut up," he said brusquely, and rather to my surprise, I did.

And there was no flippancy about me a few days later either, when I knew that Carlotta had left high school to spend the winter with an aunt in Idaho, an aunt of whom we'd never heard. I met Mrs. Berry one day when I was shopping and hardly recognized the pale, haggard woman as Carlotta's mother who had been so vivaciously excited only a few months before when Brett invited Carlotta to the prom. Mrs. Berry turned away so that she would not have to speak to me; it was a sobering moment.

There was a strange dreariness in the air that fall. At first I thought that I felt that way because of Carlotta, but later I noticed that Danny was dreary too. I didn't know why at first, but little by little, the gossip came through that he and Eden were having trouble.

Eden, it seemed, interpreted the relationship between Danny and me as being more than friendship. She didn't like it that Danny felt he must drive me into town for special events, although she was the one he squired to those events—he only gave me transportation service. She was also annoyed when he mentioned that we had ridden our horses together on some crisp autumn evening—we'd done that for the past ten years—and she didn't like it when Aunt Cordelia invited him to stay for dinner one evening after he had done some work for her.

Then Alicia and I gave a dinner party for a young foreign exchange student to which we invited Eden and Danny as well as two other couples. Eden sent her regrets, but Danny came anyway, and after that they quarreled. Eden was said to have delivered an ultimatum concerning Danny's brotherly concern for me; I could have advised her there if she had only asked me: Danny was a sweet-natured lad, but he didn't hold with ultimatums. Not at all.

And thus things stood. But if Eden (or I either, for that matter) thought that Danny would come running to me with open arms, she (and I) were mistaken. Never had I known him to be as he was that fall—silent, morose, irritable.

After a while as I looked at Danny's somber face, I

began to feel sorry for him. If he were suffering as I suffered after Brett, I felt deeply sorry for him although I was angered too, at the way he barked at me sometimes. I offered once to stop riding with him if it would help his standing with Eden, and he nearly snapped my head off. I wondered if Father had ever been sharp like that to Alicia and if she'd stood for it and what she'd done if she hadn't stood for it.

One night in November we drove out toward home in Danny's car after the last class, the last conference, the last lab make-up period any of the five of us had to attend. It was a cold, rainy evening, and the tensions aroused by term papers, love, approaching exams, lack of love, or simply the wretched weather, bore down in varying degrees of intensity upon all of us.

We deposited the three younger ones at their respective dooryards, and then Danny and I drove on through the gathering dusk together, silent, wholly uncommunicative. I remember thinking that even the windshield wipers sounded a little discouraged; their flip across the surface that was cleared one second and splashed with rain the next seemed to suggest futility and despair. "Wherefore?" they clicked wearily in one direction; and "Why?" they wanted to know as they moved in the other.

We passed Carlotta's home after a while; the place was dark except for a lighted kitchen window. I wondered about Lottie, where she was, what she was thinking that November evening. I wished that Mrs. Berry would not turn away from me when we met; I wanted very much to let her know that I would be one to welcome Lottie home when and if she returned. I wished that Mrs. Berry knew how often I said to myself: "Be very kind, Julie Trelling, be very kind in what you think and say about Carlotta."

And then Danny and I saw something at the same moment; something that made our childhood seem very far away. Carlotta's father had just thrown open the doors of his lighted garage as we were opposite it, and there, leaning a bit crazily on one side, we could see a wicker cart looking faded and decrepit even in the rainy twilight.

"The old pony cart, Danny," I whispered. Carlotta and I had never been very close, even as children, but at that moment I could have wept for her.

Danny looked at me and when he saw the tears in my eyes, he took my hand without speaking and drew my arm through the curve of his own. We sat close together, our arms locked, and the car was warm and dark and peaceful. Outside the rain splashed harder than ever against the windshield, and the wipers seemed to have drawn new energy from some source. They weren't exactly gay, but they were less despairing than they had been moments before.

We rode on like that, still silent, until we came to the long lane that led up to the house. I could see through the trees that there was a fire in the living room fireplace, that Aunt Cordelia was moving about, turning on lights and adjusting shades. The room looked inviting, but I found myself wishing that I could stay with Danny.

"You have a raincoat?" he asked. The first words in over a mile. His voice didn't sound quite natural.

"Here," I said, picking up the folded cape on the seat beside me. "Well," I hesitated. I hated to go in. I wanted to stay out there in the rain with him. But then, I thought he would probably bark at me if I suggested it. "I suppose I must dash. See you in the morning if I don't drown."

And then suddenly Danny's arms were around me, and his lips were on mine, and the crazy windshield wipers commenced singing our names together, much like the taunting of the kids in school a long time ago: Danny loves Julie; Julie loves Danny. I wondered why it had made me so fighting mad in those days.

We sat together for a long time after that, our cheeks close, our arms around one another.

"It's always been you, Julie. No one ever really except you."

"Not Eden?"

"I said 'no one ever really,' Julie. Eden is a nice girl; I liked her a lot. But she was right; I loved you, and it showed through."

I loved him so much. Without the reservations that I'd had for another boy whom I didn't like to remember. "Danny," I whispered.

"Yes, Julie?"

"I've always wanted to tell you—all these years I've been sorry about that time I hit you."

He chuckled a little. "You were a brat, but even then I thought of you as 'my girl.'"

"Was your mother mad at me?"

"No. She said that Chris and Jim and I had no right to tease you."

"My Grandmother Bishop would have scratched the eyes out of any girl who might have blacked Uncle Haskell's eye like that. He told me so."

"Not my ma."

"I love you, Danny." I felt I had to tell him. And then he kissed me again.

That was the way it was that beautiful evening of cold November rain and muddy country roads and crazy windshield wipers. That was the moment of my greatest security and confidence; it was the time when I realized that love makes one a better person, a kinder and a gentler one. I couldn't believe as I sat there in the car with Danny that I could have been jealous of Laura, that I could have been cruel to Aggie or unkind to Aunt Cordelia. Most of all I couldn't believe that I was the girl who had thought she loved Brett Kingsman.

When I finally entered the living room that evening I noticed that Aunt Cordelia had set a little table in front of the fireplace and was carrying in food from the kitchen to place upon it. This was something new for her; she didn't believe the living room was a place for eating except for coffee and cake when there were guests. Perhaps she was remembering how I had described the little suppers Alicia liked to serve in front of the fire; perhaps she was remembering that a certain pert girl had spoken of "inflexibility" as a highly undesirable trait.

"This is so nice, Aunt Cordelia," I said, taking off my wet raincape. The old room seemed to glow with beauty that night; I wondered that I had ever privately fretted over the fact that we couldn't afford to lower the ceiling or to buy a carpet handsome enough to make a proper setting for Uncle Haskell's piano.

"Well, it's such a bad night—I thought supper in front of the fire might cheer you. There's a good, rich soup tonight, and I have a souffle in the oven. We should have asked Danny to eat with us."

"Some other time," I said, seating myself in a low

chair and looking into the fire. I wanted to think quietly, to savor every sensation of peace and happiness inside me.

I noticed that Aunt Cordelia started toward the kitchen to get the souffle and then stopped in the door to look at me. She sensed something. No wonder; the whole universe was singing. But she walked away without saying anything, and returned shortly with the souffle rising high and lightly browned from the platter on which it rested.

"There is dessert in the refrigerator if you want it later, Julia. I am driving into town with Jonathan this evening. Your father and Alicia have asked us to visit them for a few hours."

I had intended telling her about Danny and me, but I suddenly decided against it. We would talk about her; I would tell her that the new crimson wool she was wearing under her big kitchen apron was becoming; I would hope that she and Jonathan Eltwing had a pleasant evening with Father and Alicia. There was no particular reason why the events of my evening should have priority over hers.

"I hope Jonathan is a careful driver," I said after a while. "It's a bad night."

Not really. Not for Danny and me. But a bad night for Father to be driving, or Mr. Peters, or Jonathan Eltwing.

Aunt Cordelia nodded. "Once when we were young, Jonathan and I drove home from town in such a rain as this. I always remembered that night—the rain and wind outside; warmth and security inside—"

It was most unusual for her to confide anything of her early years to me. I felt proud that she chose to give me a brief glimpse of something dear to her.

Then I noticed that she was smiling at me. "Didn't you find that you felt safe and happy with a good driver this evening, Julia?" she asked quietly.

"Yes," I said. "How did you know?"

"You are much like the girl I used to be," she said. "I'm glad it's Danny," she added.

Chapter Ten

Because of Uncle Haskell I had never dared admit to anyone that I had an ambition to write. If I could have suddenly bloomed in print, or if a qualified critic had praised a manuscript of mine, I could have squared my shoulders and looked any doubters in the eye. I might have asked Alicia or Father to read one of my stories; I might have asked Jonathan Eltwing, or even Aunt Cordelia, whose literary background stood up well with any of the other three. There were plenty of people to advise and guide me, but I could not bring myself to admit the fact that I was trying to write. I was sure that any such admission would bring to their minds the picture of Uncle Haskell, allegedly working for forty years on a book that no one had ever seen or was likely to see.

I wouldn't even take the evening course in creative writing which was offered in the college, and for which I, as a high school senior in honors English, was eligible. I was sure that—not my family—but everyone else who knew us, would say, "Well, well, so now it's Julie! If I were poor old Cordelia I'd lock both Julie and Haskell up in a room with two typewriters and feed them on bread and water until they produced a few thousand words between them." Something like that. And, of course, I had no more justification for believing that I could write than had Uncle Haskell. He had done well in rhetoric too, many years before, and it hadn't meant anything in particular. I wondered if I had been around him so long that I might have caught a mild case of delusions of literary grandeur.

I was often troubled by the fear that there was something of Uncle Haskell in my character; if I might possibly have certain weaknesses which had led him to become what he was. I knew that I had a tendency to be overdramatic at times; I wasn't exactly the be-good-sweet-maid-and-let-who-will-be clever type of girl. And certainly, I had always liked Uncle Haskell, not always warmly, but enough to make me seek out his companionship at times.

Perhaps the loneliness of the old house and the woods helped to foster a habit I had of peopling my mind with characters who loved, hated, despaired, and exulted before my inner eye. Alicia had said once that loneliness could be dangerous in creating so strong a need as to make a shoddy relationship seem beautiful. I wondered sometimes if loneliness had led me to dream dreams that had no basis in reality. I knew that I had a keen desire to give life to the procession of characters who walked with me through the woods or galloped beside me when I rode Peter the Great along the quiet countryside; still I didn't know whether my attempts to give them life held promise or were only ridiculous.

"Your head is in the clouds tonight, Julie," Danny would say to me sometimes, and I wanted to tell him all about my secret efforts and hopes. But might it not give Danny pause if he thought I was a female counterpart of my uncle? I would put my dreams aside against the day when Danny would read my work and be ever so proud of me.

We noticed a change in Uncle Haskell during the autumn of my last year in high school. The signs of age, so long apparently held in abeyance, seemed to appear suddenly in many little ways. Lines of fatigue or possibly, pain, showed up around his mouth; his eyes looked tired, and what was most unusual, he was given to long periods of silence. He still made an occasional trip to the banks of the creek with the old golf bag over his shoulder, but they were less frequent. For some reason his intake of *Le Vieux Corbeau* had diminished; so too, it seemed, had his gourmet's taste for his own cookery. There was a trace of wistfulness in the way he asked Aunt Cordelia if he might eat with us for a while, and there was a suggestion of humility in his appreciation for the plain but excellent meals she prepared for us.

He sought me out often during these early autumn days, and we would walk arm in arm through the bright woods, saying little, yet consciously fonder of one another, I believe, than we had ever been before. I noticed on these walks that the old buoyancy of his step was gone, that he walked slowly and deliberately; I noticed too, how his bright hair had become dulled by gray. He had always seemed at least ten years younger than Aunt Cordelia, but that fall he looked older.

One evening as we walked, I remember that he spoke quite suddenly and irrelevantly. "The old piper is clamoring for his pay these days, Julie."

I was perplexed. "I don't understand, Uncle Haskell," I answered.

He laughed, but less lightly than in other years. "Do you remember how we once discussed the state of my liver when you were little? You were entranced by a new word, and you asked me very directly if my liver was impeccable." He chuckled at the memory. "Well, it's no longer impeccable, Julie. As a matter of fact, the doctor tells me that my luck has run out. Cirrhosis."

I stopped in the path and looked at him. "Surely the doctors can do something, can't they, Uncle Haskell?"

"Apparently not. You see, I didn't aspire to just a *slight* touch of cirrhosis; I did a magnificent buildup."

To say that I was sorry seemed so trite, so inane. I was more than sorry; I don't think that even Uncle Haskell knew how desolate I felt at that moment.

Neither of us spoke for a long time. Then, when the silence became too much for me to bear, I told him of my wish to write.

It seemed callous when I thought of it later, a self-centered remark worthy of Uncle Haskell himself as it came in the face of what he had just told me. But any words of sympathy that I had were too empty, too inadequate; this was a little something I had to offer him for the grim days ahead, a something that I instinctively felt he would love.

"I've been trying for a long time to write a little, Uncle Haskell. I've never told anyone, and I'm telling you in confidence. I've wondered if you would read some of my stuff and criticize it for me? I warn you, it isn't very good, but I'd like to know if there is *any* good in it, and what I can do about what's bad in it."

There it was. I hadn't wanted to tell anyone—certainly not Uncle Haskell—about my ambition, but it seemed to have been drawn from me by an urgent necessity.

The obvious delight that came into his eyes was worth relinquishing my secret. He cut our walk short and asked me to bring him one of my manuscripts immediately. Later that evening when Danny and I walked past the carriage-house apartment on our way to saddle our horses for a ride, we saw Uncle Haskell sitting at his table, his glasses astride his nose, a sheaf of papers in his hand.

The manuscript I gave him was not my first, but I considered it at all odds to be my best. I had an old German musician telling the story of his youth, his sufferings in a cold, rat-infested attic where he composed his music. His one solace, other than his work in this desolate environment, was the beautiful daughter of his landlord. This girl, who listened enraptured to the young man's music and poured out a chaste and gentle passion for the young musician himself, was unfortunately the child of a most brutal and sadistic father who, in a story of four thousand words, wrecked the lives of all the characters involved. The musician, old and feeble, at the end of the story, had apparently had very few satisfactions in life since his criminally insane landlord went on that last rampage so many years before.

When I came home that night I found my manuscript encased in a neat manila folder and propped against my door. The outside of the folder was covered with Uncle Haskell's beautifully flowing handwriting; at the bottom of his comments he had given me a B minus.

Seated at my desk, I read his criticism:

Dear Julie:

If I didn't feel that there is some good in your story, I wouldn't take the time to write a criticism of it. But there *is* some good in it, some points that make me feel that if you expend the effort (Look who's talking about expending effort, I couldn't help thinking) you may well achieve your very worthy ambition.

First of all, you have an ear for cadence. Your sentences flow rather smoothly, and the continuity of your paragraphs is quite good.

Secondly, your imagery is sharp and clear-cut. I could *smell* that dank, rat-infested attic, and I was more than a little in love with your pretty heroine by the time she emerged from her third paragraph. Furthermore, you occasionally achieve poetic effects which are pleasing.

But, my darling niece, your villains have nothing but venom in their souls, and your sympathetic characters are ready to step right off into Paradise without one spot to tarnish their purity. People aren't like that, Julie. Take a look around you.

Again, all your colors, your moods, your nuances, are essentially feminine, and it just doesn't ring true to be told that a man is responsible for them. No, Julie, it will be a long time before you speak and think and feel like an anguished old German musician of eighty! And, after all, what do you know

about the problems of musical composition, or the
life of an impoverished German laborer such as the
landlord in his nineteenth century environment?
And how much do you know about sadism and
brutality?

I must talk to you about any number of points.
When you get home from school tomorrow, I shall
have some recommendations to make; also some as-
signments. I am quite excited. It well may be that I
have the making of a future writer in my hands.

Uncle Haskell.

I laid the manila folder aside thoughtfully. If I
hadn't done anything else, I had given him something
to get excited about. I felt very tender toward Uncle
Haskell that night.

We had long talks about my writing in the days that
followed. "Write of things you know about, Julie; familiar, simple things that you have experienced; things
that have touched you deeply."

"But nothing's ever happened to me. I've just lived
here with Aunt Cordelia and you most of my life, I've
gone to school, visited Father—oh, sure, I'm in love
with Danny, but that's something we've grown into—
very wonderful for us, but not very exciting for the
rest of the world. How can a person who has lived as
quiet a life as I have find anything to write about?"

"Then you do have a problem. If you haven't lived
long enough to have felt anything deeply, then you
are in the same position I—as many would-be writers
are. You've nothing to say. So take up crocheting."

I thought about that business of remembering an
experience which had caused me to feel deeply, and

finally as I thought, there emerged in my mind, three little figures standing at a gate in the bright October sunlight; I heard a small girl saying, "You aren't going to live here anymore, are you?" I saw a picture of sheets on the line being wrinkled into malicious faces as the wind blew them about; I heard Laura's voice begging me to stop crying, and I heard Mrs. Peters saying, ". . . and now our pretty petticoat . . ." As I remembered these things, the old feeling of desperation seemed to climb down into my throat, and I saw the closet under the stairs, felt Aunt Cordelia's arms drawing me into her lap.

That evening I went to my room and wrote for many hours, neglecting some of my schoolwork because this paper for Uncle Haskell seemed to demand precedence.

I left it with him before I went to school the next morning, and when I came home in the evening I hurried out to discuss it with him. His face was grave as he turned the paper in his hands. "Is this the way it was, Julie? Did you really experience all this?"

I nodded, and he reread a paragraph thoughtfully. "I never knew," he said after a while. "I didn't know that children felt that deeply."

He said no more about the story, but he did not hand it back to me. "I'd like to look this over a little more," he said without explanation, and laid it aside on a pile of papers.

He was as hard a taskmaster as if he had known only long hours of toil himself, and was unable to understand others who could not live up to his rigid standards. He would make me do a paper over, pointing out a hackneyed phrase, a contrived situa-

tion, a paragraph of strained dialogue. He wanted
more and more copy, and he was very stern about my
failure to turn it in as he demanded it.

"But I have my schoolwork to do, Uncle Haskell.
I can't take a chance of getting low grades. High
marks are very important to me this year."

"Any writer who really has the fire within him will
find time to write, Julie," said Uncle Haskell with the
air of a man who knew that fire well. "What about
Coleridge and Stevenson, what about dozens of
others, sick in body and mind, suffering acute pain,
but still finding the energy and time to write?"

"They weren't finishing high school," I muttered.
But I worked as hard as I was able, and Uncle Haskell went over each of my offerings with meticulous
care. He would strike out clichés with impatient little
crosses, brand paragraphs with such words as "Awkward," "Illogical," "Saccharine"; now and then he
would reward me with a benevolent "Good!" or "Big
Improvement!" My spelling annoyed him occasionally.
"Good Heavens, Julie, didn't Cordelia teach you
anything?" he would inquire via his blue pencil. And
at the end of the paper, he would spell out the major
faults of my work and the qualities he found com-
mendable. He usually placed a letter grade below his
criticism; I received several C's; nothing ever higher
than a B.

"Young writers get false ideas from indiscreet
praise," he explained. "When I tell you that your
work is good, I'm not suggesting that you're Madame
de Sévigné."

Uncle Haskell must often have been in pain during
those months; his face showed the effects of suffering,
but he never mentioned it. Aunt Cordelia and Father

talked with the doctors, and all that could be done for him was done. It was not much; temporary relief from pain, Aunt Cordelia's devotion.

"Your writing is helping him more than any medicine, Julia," Aunt Cordelia told me, for we had found it necessary to include her in our secret. "In all the years, he has had no more than a flash of satisfaction out of his strange, twisted thinking. Now, I believe he feels that finally he is making some small contribution to a society he has always ignored." She watched him as he waved to us and walked away for his evening stroll. "He might have been a very good teacher—a fine man if something terribly wrong hadn't distorted him."

Uncle Haskell suggested once or twice that I send out one or two of my best things. "See how they're received, Julie. The experience can't hurt you. Anyway, every young author must commence collecting his pile of rejection slips. You had just as well make a beginning."

But I couldn't bring myself to do it. It seemed too audacious on my part; I had a feeling that I might not only receive a rejection slip but that some outraged editor might give me a sound scolding for presuming to take up his time.

Then one week in April I had a telephone call from Father. "Julie, your story is in the *College Quarterly*," he said in an excited voice. "Darling, why didn't you tell us?"

It was a day of considerable rejoicing by those who loved me most. Father called Laura and Chris; within a few hours Chris responded with a silly but very proud telegram, while Laura and Bill put through a long-distance telephone call which was still considered an extravagance, and their congratulations extended for a period far beyond the three minutes to which Aunt Cordelia and I carefully restricted ourselves when making such calls. Jonathan Eltwing felt that I had created and sustained a mood in a way that showed promise; Aunt Cordelia and Alicia were pleased. Father, who should have known better, being familiar with the best in literature, rather lost control of his enthusiasm that day. He kept finding another point in my work to praise until I became uncomfortable; I feared that it sounded a little like Grandmother Bishop praising something Uncle Haskell had written. Everyone laughed indulgently, and I felt much relieved when Father finally achieved insight into his over-reaction and said quietly, "Well, after all, I remember her from a little vegetable on up. If what she writes gets into print, it seems great stuff to me."

Only Uncle Haskell remained aloof that day. I ran over to his place early that morning, sure that he was responsible for submitting my manuscript, and anxious to talk about it. There was, however, no response to my knock, and all during the day we saw nothing of him. It was not until late evening when I was getting ready to drive into town with Danny that I saw Uncle Haskell turning into the path that led to the creek, his beret perched jauntily on his head, the golf bag without clubs slung across his shoulder.

I ran down the lane to overtake him. "When did you send my story to the *Quarterly*, Uncle Haskell? Why didn't you tell me?" I asked breathlessly.

"My dear child," he said with mock loftiness, "I had completely forgotten your little yarn. Did they publish it, really?"

"You know very well that they published it. Oh, Uncle Haskell, I've been walking on clouds today. And how I've missed you; why didn't you answer my knock?"

"I felt no desire to join the throng. I'd sooner discuss your work when we're alone." He smiled at me, but I noticed that his face looked ashen in the twilight. "Yes, I'll admit that I submitted your story. It was the right thing to do, wasn't it? You see, my judgment of work was accurate."

"I never could have done it without your help. Never."

"I like to think that, but I'm not fully convinced." He looked out toward the misty woods and sighed. "We'll talk about it—sometime later. You run along. You're going out with young Trevort, aren't you?"

"Yes, but I'll have time to walk down to the creek with you." The look of suffering on his face hurt me. "Don't you want me to come along just this once?"

He made an effort to regain his old gayety. "I do not. I reserve the right to invite guests to accompany me on my evening strolls. Tonight, you are not invited." He kissed me lightly on the forehead. "Congratulations, my sweet; your name looked very fine in print. I have felt quite proud of you all day." I stood watching him as he went down the winding path through the woods. He turned and waved just before he disappeared among the trees.

It was rather late when I came in that night. I had thought that if Uncle Haskell's light were still on, I might run over and see him for a few minutes. But his place was dark and so I prepared for the night, setting my alarm a few minutes early so that I would have time to see him before I went to school the next morning. The white suffering in his face had bothered me from time to time all evening.

My bed felt warm and safe that night as I listened to the rain falling steadily on the roof and splashing in little puddles below my window. It had been a beautiful day, full of love and encouragement. I smiled as I thought of Dr. Adam Trelling, behaving like any foolish father over a very simple story; I thought again of Danny's good-night kiss and his whisper of how happy he was at my success. Just before I slept I thought of Uncle Haskell.

Our telephone rang very early the next morning. There are people who say that what I am about to tell must be in error; that I have imagined it this way. But I know. I know very well that when the ringing of the telephone awakened me, I lay stiffly in my bed and thought: "Aunt Cordelia will answer that ring. Then there will be a time of silence. After that, she will come up the stairs, knock at my door, and she will say, "Julia, Uncle Haskell is dead."

And it happened almost that way. Aunt Cordelia knocked at my door after the short silence, and she said, "Julia, wake up, dear. Some men have found Uncle Haskell's body in the creek. They think he fell from the old bridge last night."

For several days I wouldn't go near the old carriage-house apartment, but there finally came an afternoon when Aunt Cordelia and I had to face the task of going through Uncle Haskell's few possessions, discarding what we must, putting away for no particular reason the things we could not bear to discard.

I folded the old velvet smoking jacket and the white silk shirt which he had worn the afternoon that

he became the "good golden-haired man" for little
Katy Eltwing. We packed his books and with them
two unopened packages containing bottles such as the
one that had once reminded me of bowling pins. We
found a few papers with the opening paragraphs of a
story or an article neatly typed, but never completed.
The *College Quarterly* was lying on his desk, opened
at the page where my story began. In the margin
I read, "Sharp imagery; good plot; some tendency
toward overwriting. B+."

We worked in silence for a long time, but at last I
sat down at the desk and turned toward my aunt.
"What happened, Aunt Cordelia? What distorted
him?"

She pressed both hands against her temples for a
minute; then she sat down at the desk and looked at
me without seeming to see me.

"I'm not sure, Julia; no one can ever be sure of the
forces that have shaped a character. I think, though,
that our parents—" she paused, frowning, and then
went on. "I'm not one of the school that holds parents responsible for all the weaknesses of their children, but I must say this: we had an odd pair of parents. I loved one of them, but not the other; Haskell
loved neither of them."

"I thought that Grandmother Bishop adored him."

"She did. She smothered him with adoration and
turned his father against him. Haskell resented her
bitterly."

"You loved your father?"

"Yes. Father always seemed old to me. He was
nearly twenty years older than Mama, a stern, undem-
onstrative man, but kind. Kind, that is, to most people, not to Haskell, nor to Mama in his later years.

I think he felt that she had robbed him of his first child, his only boy. When he saw Haskell overindulged and spoiled by Mama, he rejected him completely. He loved your mother and me; he had no use whatever for his son. With Mama, it was the reverse.

"There are plenty of children who could have risen above such a situation. Not Haskell. Whether there was some basic weakness of character or whether he was, as you say, distorted, we can't know. In my heart I hold my parents responsible."

We sat there thinking. I ran my hand across the smooth velvet of Uncle Haskell's jacket; I remembered his hair. There was, indeed, something of velvet and gold about him, something that Katy Eltwing's troubled mind had glimpsed. It was shoddy velvet and tarnished gold, and there lay the tragedy, for the shoddiness and the tarnish might have been prevented.

We set things to rights and packed and stored all that had value; the rest, we burned. Before we left, we drew the shades; then Aunt Cordelia locked the door and for a long time we tried to avoid looking at the place.

Chapter Eleven

"I think, Julia," Aunt Cordelia said one morning as we stood at the kitchen table cleaning silver, "that it's time you were pushed out of the nest. I think you had better plan to attend the State University next winter."

"But I don't want to leave here, Aunt Cordelia. I want to stay with you for the next four years. Danny and I have it all planned. I don't think that I could bear to leave."

"Four more years with me and you'll be as dogmatic and opinionated as I am." She actually grinned at me. I was amazed; Aunt Cordelia often smiled primly, but I couldn't remember ever seeing her grin as though she were sharing a joke with me. "Spinster aunts serve a need, but they should know when the time comes to push young nieces out on their own."

"But you would be all alone if I left you; anyway, this is my home."

She shook her head. "You must have new experiences, be exposed to new ideas, Julia. You've fallen into a pattern here; if you stay on, you'll be another Cordelia Bishop. I won't have it."

"I don't want to leave Danny," I said, near tears.

"It would be a good thing if Danny were pushed out of his comfortable little niche too. Jonathan agrees with me. I may even speak to Helen and Charles Trevort about it."

It seemed to me that she was disposing of other people on a grand scale that morning. "I thought that you were happy about Danny and me. Now, it seems you really want to see us separated."

"I *am* happy, Julia. However," she stressed the word strongly, "both you and Danny need to get out into life and give your love a test."

I felt weak inside. "If Danny would 'get out into life' as you put it, and find that he loved someone else, I would die. I know it. I would just give up and die."

"No, you wouldn't, dear. You'd go on living. It would be hard, but if your interests were wide and your life full, you would get over the pain and find a new life." She laid her hand on my arm. "Don't look so tragic. I have great confidence that four years from now I'll be getting this old place ready for your wedding—yours and Danny's."

"It's beginning to sound like an awful gamble." We finished the silver without saying anything more; when we were through I went away to walk in the woods. It was a cool day, and Aunt Cordelia made me wear a woolen stole that Jonathan had given her for Christmas; it was the color of ripe strawberries, and I couldn't help but be cheered by its beauty.

I was still reeling from Aunt Cordelia's firm line when word came that Danny had received a scholarship from the eastern university that Chris was attending. The professors in Danny's department were pleased; so were both our fathers and Aunt Cordelia. They seemed pretty callous to us during those first weeks; then we pulled ourselves together and commenced making our plans all over again.

It had been so simple before the new developments. I would stay with Aunt Cordelia in my familiar old room; Danny would continue living at home; we would drive into college together, home together, to all the college activities together. Everything together. Just Danny and Julie for at least three years; then there would have to be one year of separation while Danny did graduate work and I finished college, but when that year was finished we would be married. Now the plans called for four long years apart, both of us among strangers, a whole new way of life. It was frightening.

"Don't fall in love with someone else, Danny," I said. I tried to make it sound gay, but I was terribly in earnest.

"I'm not worried about *me;* it's you losing your head if some poet barges in on my territory," Danny said glumly.

Little by little, however, we became less fearful of the change, more aware of the fact that we *were* living in a narrow, comfortable world, and like some little old couple of eighty or so, highly apprehensive about branching off the beaten track. By the time Chris got home for summer vacation, Danny and I were ready to join him in plans for the coming year, plans that involved several trips back and forth across half the continent for holidays and special occasions together.

I wondered sometimes when I was alone what Aunt Cordelia had meant about my becoming another Cordelia Bishop. I knew that I must look a little like the girl in the picture, at least Jonathan Eltwing thought so, but I believed the resemblance ended there. I was quite sure of it until one evening when Chris and I were talking with Father and Alicia and the subject of Jane Austen came up. Father was telling us about a paper written by a girl in one of his classes, a paper bitterly critical of any and all of Austen's writings.

"I certainly think such an attitude indicates immaturity," I said severely. I had once been intensely bored by Jane Austen myself, but I supposed that all people who had lived seventeen years had progressed in their powers of discrimination.

I saw Alicia's lips twitch when she glanced at Father; neither of them would probably have said anything, but Chris never missed an opportunity to tease.

"And, by Jove, we just don't hold with the anti-Austen clique, do we, Aunt Cordelia?"

I laughed with them that evening, but the incident set me to thinking. And when, a few days later, I was caught again in an unconscious mimicry of Aunt Cordelia, I began to agree that it was time that I got out into a wider world.

It happened when Mrs. Peters brought her two small grandchildren over to visit us. They were a beautiful, winsome little pair, a girl of five and a little boy of about three. I was delighted with their large solemn eyes and their baby voices.

When I asked them their names, the little girl answered for both. "I am Peggy, and my little brother is Bobby," she told me.

I amused them with a few old toys for a time; then when they grew restless, I suggested that perhaps they would like to go out to the stable and watch me feed a lump of sugar to old Peter the Great. I lifted the small boy into his wagon, and offered my hand to the little girl.

"We'll let Robert ride, and you and I can pull him, can't we, Margaret?"

The little girl smiled at me, almost as if she understood that here was a young woman who was showing the effects of living ten years with an aunt of decided opinions.

"You didn't listen to our names," she said in gentle reproach. "I am Peggy, and my little brother is Bobby."

I glanced at Aunt Cordelia and Mrs. Peters, who sat watching us. "Another four years, Julia, and you wouldn't be able to leave unwashed dishes in the sink overnight," Aunt Cordelia remarked.

"Worse things could happen to her, Cordelia," Mrs. Peters said.

"Much worse," Aunt Cordelia agreed, "but Laura's young Julie might feel some day that her aunt was a highly inflexible person. We don't want another generation of inflexibility," she added.

She was laughing at herself as well as at me, I thought. Perhaps Aunt Cordelia was not quite so inflexible as I had once believed her to be.

Whether or not they approved of the attitudes and opinions I had picked up from Aunt Cordelia, all the members of my family were pleased that I was

named valedictorian of my class that year. Laura and
Bill and young Julie would be coming a few days
before graduation; Father and Alicia would stay at
the old house too, in order to be close to all of us.
Aunt Cordelia and I planned a supper to be served
after the graduation exercises; besides the family
there would be Jonathan, Danny's parents and Mr.
and Mrs. Peters. Chris and Danny and I took over
the task of getting things ready.

There were no half-measures with Aunt Cordelia.
Long stored bedding had to be taken out and aired,
curtains had to be laundered, walls must be wiped
down, windows washed and floors waxed. The house
was in a state of cheerful hubbub for several days as
the boys and I carried out Aunt Cordelia's orders and
were refreshed by the most appetizing meals she
could dream up for us. We were reminded of the
days when we had swept and dusted the schoolhouse
for her, but we agreed that times were happier
now; let people who have forgotten their childhood
say that the early years are the happiest, I thought.
For me, it was good to be over that stretch of the
road which was beset by half-formed anxieties and
resentments. I could now watch Aunt Cordelia glow
over the two young men whom she loved devotedly,
and I could catch her eye and know with complete
confidence that I was just as close to her. No Grandmother Bishop denied the girl of my generation.

One bright afternoon Jonathan Eltwing came in,
ostensibly for only a brief call in order to return one
of Aunt Cordelia's books, but his face glowed with
pleasure when we insisted that he stay. I tied an
apron around his generous middle, and the boys led
our venerable professor into the living room and

pointed out the windows that had not yet been washed. He must have been the Jonathan of other years that afternoon, for he laughed and teased as lightly as did Chris or Danny, and in the evening when we had eaten the fried chicken and fresh corn-bread Aunt Cordelia prepared for us, he led the singing that continued for over an hour as the five of us sat around the table. That afternoon and evening would be a picture to remember, I thought; something precious to hold when I would be out in the world viewing the new horizons and wider vistas that Aunt Cordelia felt that I must experience.

The spotlessly clean old house was filled with family on the day before my graduation. In the library we had a few small logs blazing in the fireplace; we didn't really need a fire, but I persuaded the boys that the wind drifting in from the woods still carried a slight chill that was sure to grow sharper by evening. So they built the fire for me, knowing very well that I wanted it for beauty rather than for comfort, calling me Emily Dickinson and asking me if I'd heard of people in some far-off places freezing for want of the fuel that I was wasting. Actually, the added warmth was not unpleasant, and the glow of the flames did much to soften the aging shabbiness of Aunt Cordelia's library. We had waxed the floor and washed the windows, but the faded paper on the walls and the rows of worn bookbindings could not be bright-ened by either soapsuds or wax.

Jonathan approved of my fire. We stood before it, hand in hand, as we watched the play of the flames. "Firelight does for an old room like this what wisdom does for an old face, Julie. It softens the grimmer as-pects and compensates for the drained color."

"Doesn't goodness do the same thing, Jonathan?" I asked, looking across the hall at good Mr. Peters, who stood talking to Chris.

"That's the kind of wisdom I am talking about. Learning isn't always enough, you know. I've seen some very unlovely old faces that belonged with very well-stocked brains. There were the ones that lacked the other elements of wisdom—kindness, compassion, a sense of humor."

Alicia came in through the open door, hand in hand with my little niece. "What are you talking about?" she asked, smiling. "You have something of a high school commencement look about you. You weren't, by chance, telling Julie that it is her generation that must carry the torch that is being thrown to them tonight, were you, Jonathan?"

"No, I realize that the torch passes from one set of hands to another almost before you get the state records settled, Alicia."

Alicia nodded agreement. She looked at me, and I could see her quick eyes taking in every detail of my dress, my hairdo, even the color of my lipstick. She seemed to approve of me.

"I'd better go up and find Laura," I said. "Aunt Cordelia made her promise to hear my speech so I won't fumble it."

I noticed Father standing alone at one of the living room windows as I started to go up to my room. It struck me that he looked a little wistful that evening, a little less youngish, less animated. I noticed that the flags of gray above his temples were becoming wider and whiter lately; it didn't seem right. I went over and linked my arm in his and I noticed that his face lighted as if he were pleased.

"What were you thinking about over here by yourself, Professor Trelling?" I asked.

"About my littlest one. Forgive a cliché, Julie?"

"I'll work on it."

"Well, then it seems only yesterday—" he laughed a little and left the sentence unfinished. "I'm torn between gratitude to Cordelia and envy of her. I've never known you well enough, Julie."

"Why, we've had wonderful times together, Father. Remember how I used to love going out to dinner with you? Remember the fun we had when you and Alicia took the boys and me to New York?"

He nodded. "That's what I was thinking about, Julie. I've been a source of entertainment; I've been a father who was with you when everything was going smoothly. But I haven't been with you when you were troubled—when the crises came up. It's been Cordelia who has stood by you in those times."

Once I had said the gist of that to Aunt Cordelia. I had called Father and Alicia "holiday parents." I tried to make light of the idea now.

"The next crisis that I stumble into, I'll come running to you, Father; depend upon it." I pressed my cheek against his. "Don't be a dope, darling, you have no idea how proud I am of you," I whispered.

He smiled. "You've grown up too fast to suit me, Julie," he said. He kissed me before I ran off to join Laura.

I didn't need to practice the speech, and Laura didn't insist. We just sat together at my window, and talked of little things. We were two young women, both of us in love, and it was a time of quiet happiness and relaxation. I wished that I could marry Danny the next day and move into a cottage next to

Laura and Bill and live happily the rest of our lives.

"Do you agree with Aunt Cordelia that Danny and I should be separated—that we should get out into life and have new experiences?" I asked her.

"Yes, Julie, I do. I know it isn't what you want to hear, but I think Aunt Cordelia is right, dear."

"I've worked so hard getting up to this plateau; now it seems I have to start out on another climb."

"One never stops climbing, Julie, unless he wants to stop and vegetate. There's always something just ahead."

Then there was a knock at the door. "Girls," Aunt Cordelia's firm voice called, "we must get ready to drive into town. You and William and little Julie will go with Adam and Alicia, Laura. I suppose you will want to go with Danny, Julia."

Graduation exercises are always much alike, dreadfully routine, really, except for the members of that long processional, each one trembling a little beneath his academic robe when the first sound of the organ announces that "This is It." For those trembling ones and for the bright-faced relatives in the audience, each commencement is unique and wonderful. Alicia was jaded with many such ceremonies, but even she admitted to a special thrill that night when the long line of us walked solemnly down the middle aisle of the auditorium, and when Ned Lawrence as salutatorian and I as valedictorian took our places on the stage beside Dean Evans and my dear old Jonathan Eltwing, who was to deliver the commencement address. I remember looking down from the platform into their faces: Laura with her great blue eyes suspiciously bright as if a film of tears might be in them; Bill whispering to small Julie, both of them looking at me while she nodded to what he was whispering and clasped and unclasped her hand in a surreptitious wave. Then there were Father and Alicia, holding hands and smiling up at me; there was Christopher with his arms folded, trying to look very serene and detached, while Danny nervously and quite openly chewed at a thumbnail, a gesture which I knew would continue until he was convinced that I wouldn't collapse when it was time for me to speak.

Finally, there at the end of the row was Aunt Cordelia, stiffly erect, poised, confident that no niece of hers could do other than well in this maiden speech. "Oh, Aunt Cordelia, how funny you are. And how I love you!" I said to myself. She wouldn't have approved of such a childish thought; she would have expected me to be high-minded, reaching for the stars—that sort of thing.

I had dreaded the first few seconds of my speech just a little, that brief interval between the final words of the introduction and the sound of my own voice going out to several hundred people in the silent auditorium. But once on my feet and accustomed after a few seconds to the sound of my voice, I stood relaxed and confident, my notes at hand in case of panic, perhaps a trace of something inherited from Uncle Haskell helping to give me a sense of pleasure and well-being.

It was not a speech that was going to shake the world, but it was direct and earnest. I saw Father nod once or twice at an idea I brought out, and Danny was able to clasp his hands around one crossed knee and to give the impression of a young man entirely confident that his girl was doing all right. When I was through I had the pleasure of hearing applause ringing throughout the auditorium and of seeing Jonathan smiling at me as if I were someone very special to him.

Beautiful hours move so quickly. The speeches were applauded, the diplomas handed out, the triumphant recessional march completed, and then it was over except for the extended hands, the pleasant words of many kindly people. I walked through the crowded lobby of the auditorium, my left hand clasped tightly with Danny's, happiness in every fiber of my being.

We were almost to the exit when we stopped to stand for a minute with Aunt Cordelia, and as we stood there I saw Jonathan Eltwing making his way toward us. He took my hand in both his own.

"You did beautifully, Julie, it was a good speech." Then he turned to my aunt and offered his arm to her. "Cordelia, you have every reason to be proud."

Aunt Cordelia was never one to lose her poise. She laid her hand on the arm of this man she had once loved, one whom I rather guessed that she still loved, and her voice was coolly proper and matter of fact.

"I am, Jonathan," she said, "within certain limits, I am quite proud of her."

Tempo Classics

☐	17150	**JUNGLE BOOK** Rudyard Kipling	$1.50
☐	16974	**KIDNAPPED** Robert Louis Stevenson	$1.95
☐	17256	**LITTLE WOMEN** Louisa May Alcott	$2.25
☐	16069	**PETER PAN** J. M. Barrie	$1.25
☐	17238	**REBECCA OF SUNNYBOOK FARM** Kate Douglas Wiggin	$1.75
☐	17148	**THE SWISS FAMILY ROBINSON** Johann Wyss	$1.50
☐	17136	**TOM SAWYER** Samuel Clemens	$1.50
☐	17121	**TREASURE ISLAND** Robert Lewis Stevenson	$1.50
☐	17188	**THE WIND IN THE WILLOWS** Kenneth Grahame	$1.50
☐	17134	**THE WIZARD OF OZ** L. Frank Baum	$1.95

Available wherever paperbacks are sold or use this coupon.

◆ **ACE TEMPO BOOKS**
P.O. Box 400, Kirkwood, N.Y. 13795

Please send me the titles checked above. I enclose $_____.
Include $1.00 per copy for postage and handling. Send check or
money order only. New York State residents please add sales tax.

NAME_____

ADDRESS_____

CITY_____STATE_____ZIP_____

T-01

Tempo Classics

☐ 17048	**ALICE IN WONDERLAND**	Lewis Carroll	$1.25
☐ 16968	**AESOP'S FABLES** $1.95		
☐ 15684	**BLACK BEAUTY**	Anna Sewell	$1.95
☐ 17338	**THE CALL OF THE WILD**	Jack London	$1.95
☐ 17323	**A CHRISTMAS CAROL**	Charles Dickens	$2.25
☐ 14596	**CAPTAINS COURAGEOUS**	Rudyard Kipling	$1.50
☐ 17015	**DR. JEKYLL AND MR. HYDE** Robert Louis Stevenson $1.95		
☐ 17104	**THE GLASS SLIPPER**	Eleanor Farjeon	$1.50
☐ 17339	**HEIDI** Johanna Spyri $1.95		
☐ 17108	**HUCKLEBERRY FINN**	Samuel Clemens	$1.50
☐ 14151	**THE ILLUSTRATED NIGHT BEFORE CHRISTMAS** Alicia Austin $1.95		

Available wherever paperbacks are sold or use this coupon.

ACE TEMPO BOOKS
P.O. Box 400, Kirkwood, N.Y. 13795

Please send me the titles checked above. I enclose $_____.
Include $1.00 per copy for postage and handling. Send check or
money order only. New York State residents please add sales tax.

NAME_____

ADDRESS_____

CITY_____ STATE_____ ZIP_____

T-02